Thick Gurlz 'N Thugs

By: Lady Lissa

By: Lady Lissa

Prologue

Nikola

As I stared at my reflection in the full-length mirror, I was happy with the image that stared back at me. I smiled at the image because I couldn't believe how beautiful I looked. I also couldn't believe that I was getting married in a matter of one hour. After everything that I had been through in my past, I was finally going to marry the man of my dreams. Charles and I had been dating for almost a year and a half. After dating him for only six months, he got down on one knee and proposed. Of course, I said yes. Charles was everything I could've hoped for in a man.

He was tall, good looking and he loved me. What more could I have asked for? My love for Charles grew stronger over the past six months because I was planning our wedding. He had been working a lot of overtime to pay for this wedding, so I wanted to give him his money's worth. I hired a wedding planner because I wanted everything to be absolutely perfect. I wanted to marry Charles because I loved him. But more than anything, I just wanted to be a wife.

As I stared at my curvy body and voluptuous bosom, I could almost hear my mom's negative words in my ear. She would always say, "If you don't lose some weight, no man is gonna want you." Or, "They say the way to a man's heart is through his stomach, but how is that gonna work if that's the same way to your heart?" My mom never missed an opportunity to tell me how big I was, even though she knew how hard I had tried to lose weight. Weight was always easy to put on, but hard as hell to come off.

"Oh Nikki, you look so beautiful!" Trinity said as she smiled at me.

"You think so?" I asked.

"Girl, I know so! You are working that dress!" Trinity was my best friend in the whole world. I used to have another best friend, but that's for another time.

"You don't think it makes me look fat?" I asked.

"Girl bye! Now, you know if that dress made you look anything less than amazing, I wouldn't have allowed you to buy it. You look beautiful and your dress fits you fabulously!"

She reached in for a hug as I sniffled. "Stop it before you make me ruin my makeup," I said.

All of a sudden, we heard footsteps coming up the stairs. It sounded like a stampede. The first thought that came to my mind was that they were coming to tell me that Charles wasn't here. Our wedding was supposed to start in half an hour, so I prayed that wasn't the case.

"Nikki! Nikki!" said a breathless Tina, who happened to be one of my bridesmaids.

"What?! What's wrong? Charles isn't here yet, is he?" I asked in a panicked tone.

"Girl calm down. Of course, Charles is here," she said.

"Whew! Thank God!" I said as I breathed a sigh of relief.

"But, so is..." Before she finished telling me who else was here, my heart plummeted.

"Nikola," my mom said as she walked through the door. Oh God! My worst fears had come true. My mom was here to put a bad spell and ruin my day.

Even though I had invited my mom to my wedding, I didn't do it because I wanted her here. Of course, I didn't want her here. She was way too judgmental and negative. When she said she would be at the wedding, a smile shown on the outside. But deep down, I had hoped that on her way over she would get struck by lightning or something. Shit, anything would've been better than her being here right now.

As she walked over to me, I could tell that her smile was forced. She spread her arms as wide as she could. "I'd hug you, but my arms can only go so far," she laughed. "You look," she paused. "You look just like that big ass white limo I saw parked at the curb."

Immediately, I felt my emotions building. I could feel the lump in my throat and the tears wanting to fall from my eyes as they brimmed to the surface. Trinity ran over, grabbed some tissues and started dabbing at my eyes. Then she turned to my mother and glared at her.

"Ms. Rose, I'm gonna need you to take it down a notch please." Trinity said with attitude in her voice.

"Take what down a notch?" my mother asked. She was either totally oblivious to how she was making me feel or she just didn't care. She was my mom, so I refused to believe that she didn't care about my feelings.

"We don't want you upsetting Nikki on the biggest day of her life..."

"The second biggest day! This ain't her first time putting on a white dress," my mom said. I couldn't believe she was being that insensitive on my day.

"Ms. Rose, please!" Trinity said. "I don't want Nikki to start crying because then her makeup will be ruined. We don't have the time to redo it before the wedding starts, so please... can you be a little more sensitive to your daughter's feelings?"

"Well, I didn't say she was ugly! Just because she's as big as a double decker bus in New York City, don't mean she ain't beautiful!" my mom said.

"She's very beautiful," Tina interjected as Trinity nodded.

"Y'all so protective of my daughter. I think she's big enough to defend her own self, don't y'all think?" she asked as she started laughing.

"Ms. Rose, do me a favor. Please join the other guests in the courtyard so Nikki can finish getting ready?" Trinity said with a forced smile.

"Join the other guests? I'm not just any guest... I'm her mother!" my mom fussed. "I came to walk Nikki down the aisle."

"Wh-wh-what?" I asked as my lips trembled.

"I didn't just come to your wedding to 'join the other guests'. I came to walk you down the aisle. I mean, your father is dead, so who else gon' give you away?"

"I planned to walk by myself."

"What? What kind of shit is that?"

"That's how things are done these days Ms. Rose. It's a sign of a woman's independence when she walks herself down the aisle," Trinity said.

"That's some bullshit! She ain't independent if she getting married. All that independence about to fly right out the window as soon as she says I do to that man!" My mom turned her attention to me and asked, "Don't you want me to walk you Nikki? I mean, it might look a little strange since I'm small enough to look like the number one and you'd look like double zeros. Shit, we'd look like the number 100, but I'm still your mother."

I had heard enough.

"Excuse me," I said and brushed past everyone on my way to the restroom. I had tried my best not to let my mother's words get to me, but I couldn't hold back the tears any longer.

I stood in front of the mirror and tried to brush my tears away before they fell. I couldn't afford to ruin this makeup job on my face. I just didn't understand why my mom had to be so mean to me. Today was my wedding day for Christ's sake! This was supposed to be a happy occasion for me. I was nervous enough about getting married, and now I had to deal with my mother.

KNOCK! KNOCK! KNOCK!

"Are you alright Nikki?" asked Trinity from the other side of the door. I unlocked the door for her to come in. She took one look at my face and frowned. "Aw, don't cry sis. Just ignore your mom because she doesn't know what she's talking about. You are beautiful and this is your day. Don't let her ruin your happiness!"

"Where is she?" I asked as I dabbed at my tears. "Please tell me that she decided to leave."

"Unfortunately, she's still here. I sent her downstairs to the courtyard. Speaking of which, we need to get down there before Charles thinks you stood him up," she said with a smile.

"Right." I took one last look at myself in the mirror. Trinity was right... I was beautiful and this was my day. "Let's go!"

We grabbed our bouquets and headed downstairs. As the music started, the bridesmaids began their walk down the aisle. The groomsmen and Charles were already standing at the altar. Once my six bridesmaids had walked out, I took a deep breath and prepared myself for my walk down the aisle. I prayed that things went perfectly today.

"Please Lord, if you're listening let this go off without a hitch. Let this be everything I planned it to be," I prayed.

The French doors opened up and I headed out the door. I smiled as I walked, glancing into the smiling faces of some of our guests. Judging by the looks on their faces, it would seem as if the guests agreed with Trinity... I really was beautiful. I finally made it to the halfway point where Charles came to meet me. He looked into my eyes and smiled.

"You look amazing!"

"Thank you. You look so handsome!" I gushed.

"You wanna get married?" he asked.

"Yes!"

He linked my arm through his and we walked the rest of the way together. The pastor began his opening prayer. Then he said the words I wished he wouldn't have said. "If anyone shows just cause why these two should not be married, let them speak now or forever hold their peace," said Pastor James.

He was just about to start speaking again when we heard... "I'm sorry, but I can't let this farce of a marriage take place!"

I turned to see who the male voice was and it was Jerry, Charles's coworker. I looked to Charles for answers, but all he did was smile nervously. Everyone turned in Jerry's direction as he walked toward us. "Charles, what's going on?" I whispered.

"I'm so sorry," was all he said.

Sorry? What the hell was he sorry about? What the hell was going on? This was supposed to be one of the happiest days of my life, but it wasn't.

"I'm sorry Nikola, but you can't marry Charles," Jerry said as he looked at Charles.

"What's going on?" I asked.

"Do you wanna tell her or should I?" Jerry asked.

"Jerry, don't do this," Charles said.

"Do what? What is going on?" I repeated.

The guests were starting to snicker and whisper, and it was beginning to get embarrassing. As I stood there with a red face, I watched Charles and Jerry exchange looks that were confusing to me. Tears sprang to my eyes as I wondered what was going on.

"Jerry, don't do this! Not right now!" Charles repeated.

"I'm sorry, but I won't keep this secret any longer!" Jerry said.

The crowd of people gasped at once and then they started whispering again. Some were even laughing which made me think that everyone knew something that I didn't know. What came out of Jerry's mouth next almost caused me to pass out.

"Charles is gay!" Jerry said.

I heard the words. I saw the two of them staring at each other. I heard the snickers from the guests. But I couldn't believe what Jerry had just said. Charles wasn't gay! This had to be some cruel joke.

I placed my hand on my chest and swallowed hard. "What?" I asked in a voice barely above a soft whisper.

"Charles is gay! I'm sorry to have to do this like this, but..."

"I'm not gay!" Charles said.

"Oh right," Jerry said as her pursed his lips together while batting his eyelashes. "Well, let's try this since he's still in denial. Me and Charles have been fucking for the past nine months!"

"What?" I repeated as my lips began to tremble. I looked at Charles because I wanted to hear him say that Jerry was lying. I needed to hear him say that. I needed him to punch Jerry's lights out for trying to fuck up our big day, but he didn't.

"That's not true," he said. But there was something about his demeanor and mannerisms that made me believe that he was lying. Nine months? He had been involved with a man for nine months? How did I not know?

"Damn! Do I really have to get specific up in here?" Jerry asked in typical dramatic fashion. "Okay, in literal terms, Charles has been bending it over and I've been fucking him! Now that is the truth!"

Charles tried to speak, but I guess his words were stuck. I didn't need him to say anything because his facial expressions said it all. How did I not see this coming? The late nights. The change in attitude. The lack of sex, which I attributed to nerves for our upcoming nuptials. The wardrobe changes. It all made sense now.

WHAP!

"You son of a bitch! This whole time I have been planning this wedding, you've been fucking someone else behind my back? And not just anyone... A FUCKING MAN!!"

I was so damn mad I had to slap his ass again.

WHAP!

"I can't believe you did this to me!" I cried as I rushed back down the aisle.

"NIKOLA!!" Charles called after me, but I kept running. I had absolutely nothing to say to that man. He had ruined my special day in one of the most embarrassing ways. I never wanted to see Charles Henry again in my life.

The tears that I had been holding back finally escaped my eyes as soon as I entered the building. I was having a hard time breathing as I headed for the stairs. I couldn't even have dreamt up some bullshit like this happening to me today. I had said a prayer right before I walked down the aisle. I had begged God to let this marriage happen. I just knew that he wouldn't let me down this time, but guess what... he failed me.

Why did God hate me so much?

"WHY GOD?! WHY WOULD YOU DO THIS TO ME AGAIN?!" I asked as I rushed into the restroom and locked myself inside.

How would I ever be able to look people in their eyes again without feeling the embarrassment of today? Why couldn't I just find someone to love me for me? At this point, I was just ready to give up on love.

Chapter one

Nikola

That was one of the most embarrassing moments of my entire life and I've had plenty of those in the past. I couldn't believe Charles had been sleeping with Jerry's ass... literally. How could he have done that to me knowing what happened in my last relationship?

KNOCK! KNOCK! KNOCK!

"Nikki, are you okay?" asked Trinity from the other side of the door.

What the hell kind of question was that for her to be asking me right now?

"NIKKI!" she called out as she banged on the door.

"Of course, I'm not okay Trinity! Weren't you just out there?" I asked. "Didn't you just witness me getting stood up at the altar because the man I was supposed to marry is fucking another man?! Oh my God! How could this be happening to me?"

I hated snapping at my best friend because I knew she meant well. I just couldn't understand how she could even fix her mouth to ask me that question. Was I okay? Hell no! I wasn't okay now and I might not ever be. How could I show my face around town again after what just happened? We had invited 175 guests to attend a wedding that never happened. All those people knew that my husband was playing the muddy booty game now. That was even more embarrassing than me being left at the altar.

"Open the door Nikki please!"

"Go away Trinity please! I just wanna be left alone."

"Nikola! Nikola come out here please! We need to talk about this!" Charles said as he banged on the door.

Oh no, he didn't just bang on this damn door after humiliating the shit outta me! I just knew that triflin' ass nigga wasn't on the other side of the door after what he had just done to me. I rushed to the door and pulled it back angrily. Sure enough, there he was... along with Trinity, my mother and a couple of other bridesmaids with concern written all over their faces.

"You ladies can go home! There's no sense in sticking around when there isn't going to be a wedding!" I said with a tight-lipped expression while looking at Charles. When I said tight-lipped, that's exactly what I meant too. My lips were closed so tight together that my mouth was beginning to hurt.

"Please let me talk to you," Charles begged. "It wasn't like what you think."

"Were you sleeping with Jerry?"

"Can we talk in private please?" he asked.

"Talk in private? Your lover just blasted your sexual relationship in front of all the guests AT OUR WEDDING!! Why do we need to talk in private?" I asked.

"This isn't anyone else's business but ours..." Charles said.

"Shit, that's a damn lie! Everybody knows what you been doing with that queer!" my mom blasted. "You been bending over so that other faggot could plug up yo ass with his ding-a-ling?! Now you wanna talk to my daughter about that bullshit! You ain't talking to her about a damn thing!"

Everybody gasped as all eyes turned to her. "What? What the fuck are y'all all looking at me for? I just said what everybody else was thinking!"

She was right. What did Charles and I have to discuss? We should've been had this discussion and called off the wedding if all of that shit had been taking place. Why would he play me like that when he knew how my engagement ended the first time? That's right, this was the second time I was supposed to get married and it didn't happen. Why would Charles do me that way in front of all my family and friends?

"I have nothing to say to you Charles! I suggest you get the hell out of my face before I really explode up in here!" I said.

"Look Nikki, I know you're upset…"

"UPSET?!" I said loudly as I chuckled. "YOU THINK I'M UPSET?! NIGGA I'M BEYOND UPSET!! I'M FUCKING LIVID!"

"And you have every right to be!" he said as his whole body trembled. Shit, he probably thought I was gonna hit him again. If he kept pushing me, I might just have to hit him one more time.

"You damn right she does! Just tell me this… why the hell did you propose to my daughter if you was out there fucking some man?!" my mom asked.

"Ms. Rose, please…"

"Naw nigga! Don't please me! I think you owe us all an explanation!"

"Nikola, can we please speak in private?" Charles asked with pleading eyes.

"NO! Your time to speak to me has expired. You should've spoken to me last month, last week, hell… you could've spoken to me last night! But instead of coming clean about your affair, you let me think that we were going to have a wedding. You let me think that we were going to be married and live happily ever after. Then your lover shows up and embarrasses me in front of all those fucking people! Did you even think about how that would make me feel to have this happen to me on MY WEDDING DAY?!" I asked as tears slid down my cheeks.

I was not going to do this with him right now. I wasn't going to let him see how badly he had hurt me. I quickly brushed the tears away from my eyes.

Anytime would've been a bad time to find out that the man I loved and planned to marry was dipping in the muddy waters. But no time was worse than right now! He let me put on my wedding dress. He let me walk down the aisle. He let me stand with him at the altar, knowing that his lover was in attendance.

"I'm sor..."

Before he could finish, I held my hand up to get him to shut the fuck up! I didn't believe for one minute that he was sorry because a sorry person wouldn't have done me like that.

"Please don't fix your mouth to apologize to me! If you're sorry, it's because yo ass got caught! Now, get the fuck out of my face and stay the hell out of my life! I never want to see or hear from you ever again!" I said as I lifted my dress and made my way down the stairs.

"WHERE ARE YOU GOING?!" Trinity yelled at my retreating back.

"Some place where I can be by my damn self!" I said as I walked out the door.

I had no idea where I was going, but I hopped in the awaiting limo anyway. I looked at the clock on the dashboard and realized I still had two hours for the use of this ride.

"Where to ma'am?" asked the driver.

"Can we please just drive?" I asked as I shut the door.

"Don't you wanna wait for your groom?" he inquired.

"Just get me as far away from here as possible please!"

"Yes ma'am!"

He maneuvered the car onto the busy street and headed toward the French Quarter. I guess he thought a little noise would help me deal with what happened. I didn't know where I wanted to be right now. I just knew that I couldn't be with Charles ever again. He was sleeping with Jerry! Just the thought of Charles sharing my bed with me after sleeping with a man made me wanna vomit. I mean, what would make him turn to a man after being with me?

I couldn't even ask if I wasn't enough woman for him because he definitely didn't want a woman. I wanted to cry my eyes out, but that wasn't the way to handle this situation. I wasn't going to curl up in a ball and hide beneath the covers for days the way I did when Miles ended things with me.

The driver turned on Decatur and I spotted a blues club.

"STOP!" I called out.

He stopped the car. I handed him a tip and stepped out of the car. I turned a few heads walking down the sidewalk in a wedding dress.

"Ma'am, you forgot your veil!" the driver called out.

"Throw it away!" I said and kept walking.

I walked into the club around three that afternoon. Of course, all the heads turned, and all eyes were on me once I walked inside the bar too. People acted like they never saw a bride before. I guess I was as beautiful as Trinity said I was, but damn. I strutted to the bar not caring what they thought about me. I hadn't come here for their stares or opinions. I didn't even know why I was here, but the music was very nice. I headed to the bar and sat on one of the barstools. Immediately, the bartender walked over to me for my order and some unwanted banter which I didn't need.

He stared at me for a few minutes without asking for my order or anything. Like what the fuck!

"Uh, why are you just staring at me like that? Do you want my order or not? Cuz I thought this was a bar!"

"I'm sorry for staring like that. What can I get you?" he asked while wiping a glass.

"Can I please get a shot of Patron? Make that a double shot!" I said.

He grabbed a shot glass and placed it on the bar. He poured Patron in the glass and put the bottle down. I picked up the glass and downed the contents in one swift gulp. The clear, warm liquid was smooth going down, but made my body shake a little. I placed the glass on the bar and raised my finger another shot. He poured another one and I drank it while he stood there with the bottle in his hand.

"Another," I said.

"Do you think it's wise for you to be drinking so much? I'm just saying that this drink might taste good going down, but when it hits you, it may knock you off your feet," he said.

"Look, while I appreciate your concern, as you can see I'm a big girl. That means I can handle myself and my alcohol!" I said with an attitude.

"Yea, but..."

"Isn't it your job as bartender to tend to the bar? I'd like another shot please!"

He nodded his head and poured another one in the small glass. I downed that shot as well. My head was beginning to spin, so I ordered a Shirley Temple. I paid the bartender, took the drink and went to sit at a table in the corner. I sat and listened to the music being played live by the blues band on stage.

As I sat in the corner nursing my drink, the day's events played in my head. I couldn't believe that Charles had played me that way. My whole world had been rocked once again by a man I trusted and loved. Why did God keep allowing this to happen to me? Why would he do me like this after what happened the first time with Miles?

Thinking back to that time almost four years ago made my insides quiver...

Miles and I had met through Trinity and her boyfriend Derek. Derek and Miles worked for the same welding company. I didn't know what made the two of them decide to set the two of us up, but for me it was love at first sight. Miles was tall, lean and very handsome. He had braids and neatly trimmed facial hair. I wasn't too fond about the facial hair, but once he opened his mouth and I saw his beautiful white teeth, I was in awe.

He and I talked that whole night and we went out the next night. From there, things just fell in place. One year later, Miles asked me to marry him and of course, I said yes. How could I not when I thought someone as thick as I was would never find love? I was 5'8 and weighed about 325 pounds. My weight wasn't all in my belly, but in my butt too. I had a caramel skin tone, big brown eyes, high cheekbones, and just a beautiful face. However, having a big body didn't make men flock my way. I was so excited about becoming Mrs. Miles Jenkins and planning the wedding that I missed signs that something in our relationship had changed.

One month before the wedding, Miles asked to meet me for lunch. I accepted and was sitting at the table for a half hour by myself. I thought he had stood me up for some reason. I had been praying really hard that he hadn't gotten in an accident because I had been calling him like crazy and he hadn't answered. He finally showed up, but surprisingly to me he wasn't alone. He was with some slim built, light skinned, blonde haired chick. As the two of them made their way to the table, I had this sinking feeling in the pit of my stomach that this wasn't a good sign. Who the fuck was she and why was she here?

The two of them sat down together in the booth across from me. The uneasy looks on their faces made me nervous. "I didn't know that someone else would be joining us." I said as I looked from Miles to the girl beside him. "Who is she?"

"Uhm, this is Tiffany. Tiffany, this is Nikola."

"Nikola, his fiancée!" I reiterated as I showed her the ring on my left-hand ring finger. The girl looked a bit nervous as she greeted me with a shaky smile. "So, who exactly are you Tiffany and why are you here?"

She turned her gaze to Miles, but didn't respond to my question. What the hell? Was she mute or something? I asked her a simple question.

"Well... uhhhhh, look Nikola there's no easy way to say this, so I'm just gonna spit it out. I can't marry you!" Miles said.

What the fuck did he just say to me? My hand grabbed for my chest because I honestly felt as if I couldn't breathe. What the hell did he mean he couldn't marry me? The freaking wedding was next month! How could he tell me that shit when the wedding was a month away? I had spent a lot of money on this wedding and that was money that I couldn't get back from the vendors. All the flowers, venue, food, cake, dress... everything had been decided upon and paid for. What the hell was going on and why was he doing this?

"What are you talking about Miles?" I said as I felt a lump rise in my throat. I narrowed my eyes at that bitch Tiffany because I just knew her skinny ass had something to do with this. "Are you the reason that he's calling off the wedding? Have you been sleeping with that bitch behind my back?!" I was infuriated and while I knew I should be more upset with Miles than her, I couldn't help feeling the way that I felt.

I had always felt insecure around skinny bitches, and Miles said he never understood why because I was so beautiful. But if that was true and if I was really that beautiful, why was he calling off our wedding? Didn't he realize how badly this shit would hurt me?

"Me and Tiffany are together..."

"So, she is the reason you're calling off the wedding?"

"Yea..."

"Why? Why would you do that shit to me? Everything is paid for! The wedding is NEXT MONTH!!!!" I yelled, not caring

how loud I was. People in the restaurant turned their heads in our direction as I grabbed a handful of napkins to wipe my eyes.

"Please calm down."

"CALM DOWN?! YOU WANT ME TO CALM DOWN WHILE YOU'RE BREAKING MY HEART?! ARE YOU FUCKING SERIOUS RIGHT NOW?!" I asked. I wanted to lower my voice, but I was so hurt. I couldn't believe that Miles was doing this to me.

I might have been able to talk him out of this if he hadn't brought that bitch with him. He shouldn't have brought her here. This was a private conversation between him and I, so he shouldn't have brought her. Why would he bring her into our shit? If he wanted to call off the wedding and end things with me, he should've done it with just the two of us. This shit was so embarrassing.

"Nikola, I know that this is hard, but you need to lower your voice or we're gonna leave." I decided to not say anything, so he could say what he felt he needed to say.

Everything in me wanted to reach across that table and choke the shit out of that bitch, but that would've been stupid on my part. Women who were wronged by men often lashed out at the female, but it wasn't her fault. It was his fault. He was the one who cheated on me, not her.

"I'm sorry. I didn't mean for this to happen, but we fell in love. I know that I'm wrong for not telling you sooner, but I didn't know how. I know that you're upset, but one day you *are going to realize that this was for the best. And one day, you'll find someone who can love you the way you deserve to be loved," he continued. I wasn't really trying to hear all that. He had just broken my heart in the worse way possible. He had even brought his new bitch to witness me fall apart. I wanted to say something, but the words just wouldn't come out. "I don't want you to hate me and I know you've spent a lot of money on the wedding." He reached in his jacket pocket and pulled out an envelope, then slid it across the table toward me.*

"What's this?" I asked.

"It's a check for some of the money you spent on the wedding. I felt I owed you that much."

The nerve of that bastard! But I wasn't a fool though. He was right... I had spent a lot of money on that damn check, so he did owe it to me. I wasn't about to refuse it because I needed it. I took the envelope and placed it in my purse. Then I picked up the glasses of water and sweet tea that I had in front of me and tossed them in their faces. The bitch shrieked like a damn monkey, probably because it had ruined her expensive wig. Ask me if I gave a fuck. I stood up and walked the hell out of that restaurant with my head held high.

While I put on a brave front inside the restaurant, my insides were quivering like Jell-O as I made my way outside. How could this have happened to me? As I slowly walked over to my 2018 Nissan Maxima, I cringed at the thought of Miles and that woman laughing at me. The one thing I hated to think about was the two of them lying in bed after sex talking about me.

As soon as I got inside the comforts of my car, tears began to fall from my eyes. I was beyond hurt. But I didn't want them to see me that way, so I started my car and hightailed it out of the parking lot.

That was three years ago, and here I sat on what was supposed to be my wedding day alone again. As I continued to nurse my drink, I saw a couple of hoodlums walk in the door and head to the bar. I rolled my eyes and bobbed my head to the music. A couple of minutes later, one of the thugs had the nerve to walk over to my table as if he was invited to sit with me.

"Are you enjoying the music?" he asked. I looked up at him and just rolled my eyes. "Damn! It's like that huh?"

"Excuse me, but does it look like I'm in the mood for company?"

"Maybe not, but you ain't gotta be all rude about it."

"Oh, you think I'm rude?" I asked.

"A lil bit, yea. To be honest, I just wanted to check on you. We don't get many brides in here without a groom," he said.

Was he trying to be funny?

"Wow! How nice of you to point that out to me. But peep this, you ain't gotta check up on me. Go check on someone else!" I snapped.

"Damn! You know what? I ain't even gon' trip because you're obviously going through some serious emotions since you here by yourself in your wedding dress. So, with that being said, you enjoy the rest of your night."

With that, he walked away and headed to another table. The people at that table seemed genuinely happy to see him. As he made the rounds going from table to table, it made me curious as to why he would be doing that. I mean, what thug had the time to greet strangers and why? A waitress walked over to my table to see if I needed something.

"Would you like another drink ma'am?" she asked.

I looked at my glass and then back at her. "No, I'm good." I responded in a somewhat slurred tone. She turned to walk away, but I stopped her. "Excuse me. Can you tell me who that guy is over there?"

"Which one are you referring to?"

"The one with the leather jacket," I said as I pointed to him in a sly manner. The last thing I wanted was for him to get wind that I was inquiring about him.

"Oh, that's Blaze... he owns this club," she said with a smile.

She turned and walked away, leaving me with my thoughts. How could he be the owner of this fabulous club? He looked like one of those thugs that worked for Nino Brown. Since when did they start opening blues clubs? I continued to bob my head from side to side in tune with the music as the alcohol played tricks on my mind.

I'd be lying if I said that was the last I thought of Mr. Blaze, but it wasn't. I continued to sit there as he made his rounds to the other tables. He was fine, I'd give him that. But I definitely didn't need to be thinking about no man right now. Fuck all men!

Chapter two

Blaze

When I walked into the bar, the first thing I noticed was a woman in a wedding dress sitting at a table. I wasn't shocked to see a bride in here because brides did come to the club. What shocked me was to see her by herself. That could mean one of two things happened... either her man was in the restroom or she got stood up at the altar. After watching her a few minutes, it became evident that she was alone. I instantly felt sorry for her because no one deserves to be left at the altar on their wedding day.

I spoke to Carl, the bartender to see if I could get any information about the pretty thick chick out of him. "Wassup Carl?"

"S'up boss man!" he greeted.

"The house is pretty packed tonight."

"As always."

"What's the deal with the bride over there?" I asked as I nodded in her direction with my head in an inconspicuous manner.

"Aye man, major attitude," he said.

"Oh yea?"

"Yea, I think she got left at the altar or something."

"Damn. I figured that's what happened to her when I saw her sitting alone."

"Yep, that's my guess."

"Damn! That's rough!"

"Yea, and like I said, she got that Godzilla attitude..."

"I think I'ma go holla at her."

"I wouldn't do that if I was you," he advised.

"I think I can handle her."

"Humph! Your funeral," he said with a laugh as I walked off.

As I walked over to her table, I could smell the attitude that Carl was talking about. As I said, this wasn't the first time a bride had visited my establishment. However, it was my first time seeing a bride without a groom. Figuring the worst, my heart immediately went out to her. She was a beautiful woman, and she was healthy and thick too. She had her hair done in an updo with curls hanging. She had a rich chocolate complexion, and pretty brown eyes which shined brightly under the lights. I couldn't miss the frown on her face though, nor the engagement ring on her left hand.

When I greeted her, a wall of defense immediately went up and it was very visible to me. I knew she didn't want to be bothered, but I couldn't help myself.

"Are you enjoying the music?" I asked. The look she gave me was one that would stop traffic. All of a sudden, the room felt really chilly. "Damn! It's like that huh?"

"Excuse me, but does it look like I'm in the mood for company?"

Actually, it didn't look like she wanted any company at all, but I wasn't going to give up. She was my type of woman... thick in the waist and cute in the face. Most men couldn't handle thick women like her, but I definitely could. I loved my women with some meat on her bones.

"Maybe not, but you ain't gotta be all rude about it. To be honest, we don't get many brides in here without a groom. So, I was just checking on you." That might not have been the best thing for me to say to her, but I had to keep it real.

"Well, thank you for checking on me, but now you can go check on someone else!" she snapped with a neck roll.

Damn, shawty was a firecracker! Normally, I liked a woman with a little fire in her, but this shit was too much. All I was trying to do was be friendly with her because she looked like she had a rough day, but she didn't seem interested in that shit. So, if that was her way of getting me to back off, she got her wish. I didn't have any time to waste on a woman who was clearly in her feelings. Don't get me wrong, it was definitely her right to feel some kind of way. I mean, considering it looked as if her day hadn't gone the way she had planned it, so I guess I could understand her rudeness. But, rather than keep pushing up on her, I pulled all the way back.

"Damn! You know what? I ain't even gon' trip because you're obviously going through some serious emotions since you here by yourself in your wedding dress. So, with that being said, you enjoy the rest of your night."

She wasn't going to be able to bite my head off more than once. I walked around to the other tables greeting the customers. Some of them were regulars who came in every Saturday or at least two to three times a week. Like Mr. and Mrs. Richardson, who were an elderly couple that came to the club every Saturday to listen to the band. I loved those two because they were always so happy. I always made it my business to get at least one dance with Mrs. Richardson while her husband cheered us on. At 73 and 74 years old, they were the epitome of an awesome couple. I wasn't looking for a wife just yet, but when I did marry, I hoped my marriage lasted as long as the Richardson's.

By two a.m. everyone had filed out of the club except the beautiful lonely bride. She just sat there in a daze all by herself. She looked as though she was fast asleep, but she wasn't. As I walked over to her table, her eyes glared at me through mere slits.

"Are you okay?" I asked.

"Why? Don't I look okay?"

"Not really. Do you have a ride home? I mean, we're getting ready to close up for the night," I said.

"No, I don't," she said in a softer tone.

"I could give you a ride home if you like." Her eyes popped open immediately as she glared at me. "I promise not to try anything. I'm just trying to make sure you get home safely."

"Why do you care?" she asked in a slurred tone.

"I care about all my customers."

"Well, if you really don't mind, I'd like it if you drove me home."

"Sure. Just give me one minute," I said as I headed to the bar. "Carl, make sure shit is kosher before you leave yo. I'm gonna drop shawty off at her crib then head home."

"Aight boss man. Be careful," Carl said.

"Yea, aight."

I headed back over to the beautiful, thick damsel in distress. I reached my arm out to her just in case she needed help walking. She took it and was a bit wobbly on her feet when she stood up, I held her up though. As we walked out, she leaned against me. I helped her inside my black on black Range Rover and buckled her seatbelt. I made my way around to the driver's side and started the truck.

"Nice truck," she said.

"Thanks." She then rattled off her address and I already knew where that was. I was a roadrunner, so I knew just about every street in the New Orleans area.

"Sorry I gave you such a hard time earlier."

"Not a problem."

"It's just that today was supposed to be the best day of my life, but it turned out to be the worst," she said.

"Sorry to hear that," I said.

"Thank you."

"If it makes you feel any better, you are a very beautiful bride," I said.

"Thanks."

"You're welcome."

"I'm Nikola."

"Nice to meet you Nikola, I'm Blaze," I said.

She sat quietly for a few minutes, probably thinking about her situation or so I thought until I heard her softly snoring. I imagined she had a rough day, so I didn't wake her. Once I arrived at her place, which was a luxury condominium complex, I parked my truck in an available spot closest to her number. I had driven by this place many times before, but had never actually been here. I turned the car off and gently shook her awake.

"Hmm," she said as she struggled to open her eyes.

"We're here," I said.

She didn't respond. I noticed that she had been holding on to a small white clutch all night long. I peeked inside to see if her keys were in there and thankfully, they were. I hopped out of the truck and headed to the door. I unlocked it and left the door partially ajar, then returned to the truck to help my passenger get out of the truck. I reached across her lap and unsnapped the seatbelt. I dropped her keys back in her clutch and then scooped her up out of the seat.

She was a really thick female, but nothing I couldn't handle. I shut the door and made sure the alarm on my truck was secure. I walked back up to her door and went inside, clicking the lock in place behind me. I placed her purse on the table by the door and went in search of her bedroom. She gently stirred in my arms and peeked at her surroundings.

"Mmmm! You're so strong," she marveled with a smile. "And you smell so good."

"Thanks, and you're not that heavy," I replied.

I found the bedroom and flicked the light switch on. I walked over to her king-sized bed and placed her down on top of it. "Thank you so much."

"No problem. Have a good night Nikola."

"No!" she said as she jumped up. She reached up and wrapped her arms around my neck. "Please don't leave me. I don't wanna be alone tonight."

I really didn't think she knew what she was saying. After all, she had a lot to drink and I was sure it was the alcohol talking. I gently tried to pry her hands from around my neck. "No, I don't think that would be a good idea in your condition," I said.

"Please. I just can't handle another rejection today." She said as she pouted with her head leaned up against my chest.

Dammit! Now, how was I going to say no to that? "Okay. I'll stay with you until you fall asleep."

"Thank you Blaze. Can you help me out of my dress and shoes please? I really need to use it," she said.

"Sure." She sat on the bed and I lifted her dress to remove the pretty heels from her perfectly manicured feet.

Then she stood up and turned for me to unbutton her gown. When I was done with the 50 buttons down her back, she rushed to the bathroom holding the bottom of the gown in her arms. I sat on the side of her bed with my head in my hands wondering how I got myself in this situation. Of course, I knew how. I was just being a gentleman and looking out for one of my patrons. I had no intention to stay the night with her. We didn't even know each other like that, and I wasn't one to take advantage of a female, especially one who was as drunk as she was.

If I did that, she might wake up in the morning and accuse me of some shit I didn't do. No way was I ever going to jail for no bullshit like that. She returned from the bathroom minus the dress. Instead, she had a white chiffon robe. I wasn't sure what was underneath, but I knew I needed to get outta there quick, fast and in a hurry before my dick made me do some shit I'd regret tomorrow. She looked absolutely gorgeous.

I turned my head away because I didn't want to stare at her half naked body. *I shouldn't even be here right now,* I thought as my dick began to rise.

She climbed in the bed and crawled over to where I was standing. Again, she wrapped her arms around my neck and asked, "What's the matter? You don't find me attractive?"

"Nah shawty, it ain't that. You're very attractive. I just don't want to take advantage of you in the vulnerable state you're in right now."

"You're not taking advantage of me," she slurred.

"I would be taking advantage of you when I'm aware that you're under the influence."

She pressed her lips to mine and that was an awkward moment... at first. As she moaned and stuffed her tongue inside my mouth, I found myself enjoying the kiss, so I kissed her back. At the end of the day, I'm a man and I loved women. She pulled me close as she dropped backward on the bed. Her robe opened up as we were kissing. I couldn't help myself as my hands roamed and caressed her soft, voluptuous body. Before things could go any further, I stopped and backed up a little.

She instantly pouted as she stared up at me. "Please don't reject me. I really need this," she begged. "And I need you Blaze. Please."

There was no way I'd be able to look at myself in the mirror tomorrow if I went ahead and had sex with this woman. We didn't even know each other.

She pulled me closer to her and began to kiss me again. What the hell was I supposed to do now? I kissed her deeply and hungrily on the mouth before my kisses began to travel elsewhere. I kissed and licked her neck and found my way to her breasts. She moaned as she held my head in place. I circled her meaty nipples with my tongue as she cried out in pleasure. She reached for my belt and tried to unfasten it with trembling hands.

"Are you sure about this?" I asked.

"Very sure."

I slid out of the bed and walked over to the light switch. I turned it off, but the room was still illuminated by a light shining from outside. I could see her laying on the bed watching me. I removed my jacket and shirt. Then I removed my shoes, pants and boxers. My dick was pointing straight ahead as soon as I released it. I reached for a condom and unwrapped it before rolling it onto my pipe. I said a silent prayer that God would forgive me and climbed on top of her.

At first, it was a bit awkward because I had never been with a woman of her size before. Don't get me wrong, I had nothing against a curvaceous woman. Shit, my dick was hard so that meant we liked what we saw. I just ain't never had one before until now. I finally found a position comfortable for the both of us and inserted my dick inside her.

"Oooouuu!" she moaned.

"Too much?" I asked.

"No... I'm fine," she said breathlessly.

I held her left leg up and pushed a little deeper. My dick was ten inches last I checked, so I knew I had enough to get the job done. As I rotated my hips, she moaned in pleasure. "Oh my God!"

I had never felt a softer, more squishy pussy before in my life. She made me wanna bust a nut right now, but I wasn't gon' do it. Her whole body was soft, like pillow soft and plush. As we got the rhythm matching and a steady pace going, the pleasure was something I couldn't even describe.

"Damn, you got some real good pussy," I complimented.

"Umm hmm."

The two of us engaged in sex for about an hour and a half, several different positions I might add. She was very flexible with her legs and liked to try new things. By the time I had nutted, she was exhausted and so was I. After tossing the used condom and cleaning up my dick, I returned to the bedroom to hear her softly snoring. I wasn't sure if I should lay with her or leave. On one hand, if I stayed, she'd wake up next to me in the morning and know that I was a real nigga. On the other hand, if I left, I'd look like the creep who took advantage of her.

I decided to stay, so I climbed in next to her and snuggled against her cushy body until I fell asleep. I never knew big girls were so fucking soft. I fell asleep in no time.

The next morning, I was awakened by Nikola screaming at me like I had done something wrong.

"What the hell are you doing here? In my home? In my bed?!"

Damn! Something told me that this wasn't a good idea... I should've listened.

"What?" I asked as I tried to comprehend what she was asking me. I had been sleeping good as fuck, so the last thing I expected was to be awakened by her. At least, not in that tone of voice.

Like what the fuck did she mean what was I doing in her home and bed? Shit, she begged me to stay with her last night. Didn't she remember that shit? I don't know why I was surprised though. Considering how much she had to drink last night, I would've been more surprised if she had remembered everything that went down. I was a bit disappointed though. I mean, after the dick down that I gave her, how could she not remember what happened?

As she stared at her nude body, she quickly glared at me. "Oh my God! We're naked!" she yelled.

"Uh yea!" I shook my head and wiped my eyes as I tried to get a handle on things. "Nikola, what's going on?"

"What's going on? What's going on? Why don't you tell me! Why are you naked and why are you in my bed?!"

"So, you don't remember?"

"Remember? Remember what exactly?"

"Anything that happened last night?"

"If I remembered what happened, do you think I'd be freaking out like this?" She was standing beside the bed in the robe she had on when she exited the bathroom last night. She turned her back toward me and continued her tirade. "I need you to get dressed and get the hell out of my house!"

"Look, this can all be explained if you just calm down."

"Calm down? You want me to calm down? I woke up to a naked stranger in my bed and you want me to CALM DOWN?!!" she yelled as she huffed and puffed.

Okay, well, maybe calming her down wasn't going to be as easy as I thought it would. The last thing I needed was her neighbors calling the cops on me for a misunderstanding. I knew I was taking a huge gamble by staying the night with her, but unfortunately, I let my dick speak for me. I slowly slid out of the bed and started to put my clothes on. As my semi hard dick swung, I caught her eyes taking in the view. I almost wanted to take her in my arms and give her a repeat of last night... only this time, she would definitely remember.

"You seriously don't remember how we got here?" I asked as I stepped into my boxers.

"NO!"

"Can I please explain? I don't want you to get the wrong idea about me."

"You took advantage of my inebriated and vulnerable state... that's what happened!"

"No, I promise you that if you give me a couple of minutes..."

"Just get out of my house!"

Shit, she didn't have to tell me that a third time. I had tried to explain myself to her because I didn't want her to think of me that way. I wasn't that kind of guy... the kind that would've just taken advantage of her that way. I didn't mean for things to get so out of hand.

"I'm sorry if I did anything that made you uncomfortable," I said.

"JUST GET THE HELL OUT OF MY HOUSE!!" she shrieked.

I headed for the door as fast as my legs would take me. Once outside, I breathed a sigh of relief as I quickly hopped in my truck. What the fuck had just happened? Why the fuck did she act like I did something she didn't want me to do? Shit, she wanted me and that was the only reason I stuck around last night. Dammit! I knew that shit was a mistake.

I wished she would've given me the chance to talk to her before she just threw me out. I would've never taken things as far as we did if I would've thought this would happen. I knew that she was drunk, so I should've just dropped her off and left.

Dammit! I sure hope this shit wouldn't come back to haunt me...

Chapter three

Nikola

I woke up the next morning with the worst hangover ever. I could barely open my eyes, let alone focus on where I was. As I laid in bed trying to open my eyes, I could hear the soft snoring of someone. I just knew I had to be imagining shit. It must be from all the alcohol I consumed yesterday. All of a sudden, I felt the need to throw up. I jumped out of bed and barely made it to the bathroom in time. I quickly threw myself over the toilet and vomited everything that was in my stomach, which wasn't nothing but alcohol. After I had nothing left, I flushed the toilet and headed to the mirror.

As I stared at my reflection, I didn't like what I saw. I just didn't look like the happy, confident woman I normally was. I brushed my teeth and rinsed with mouthwash. Then I washed all the makeup off my face before returning to the bedroom. Something about my body felt different though. My thighs kind of hurt and my kitty was throbbing in the worst way. Damn, it almost felt like I was in a car accident yesterday.

Ugh! Thinking about yesterday caused me to roll my eyes. Yesterday had been the worst day of my entire life... well, second worst day. As I made my way over to the bed, I heard the soft snoring sound again. Where was that noise coming from? I knew damn well Charles hadn't made his way over to my house... not after the way that we left things yesterday. I never wanted to see his damn ass again.

With that being said, I slowly turned on the bedside lamp and looked to see who the hell was snoring in my bed. As I stared at the sleeping stranger, I almost pissed on myself.

"Please tell me that is not the man from the club last night," I silently prayed. As I took a better look at him, I realized it was the same dude. I ran back in my bathroom and locked the door.

"What the hell is he doing here?" I questioned myself in the mirror. "How did he even get here? How did I get here?" As I paced the bathroom floor, I tried to wrap my brain around what happened last night. As hard as I tried, I couldn't figure shit out. I stood and leaned against the counter. "Okay Nikki, calm down. Calm down and think hard."

I took a deep breath and stared at myself in the mirror. I had to go out there and get this man out of my house. I didn't know why he was here, but this wasn't right. I walked out to the bedroom and stood tall. I wouldn't be intimidated in my house by some stranger... no matter how handsome he was. I walked over to the bed and nudged him.

"Hey," I said as I nudged him. He didn't move, so I nudged him again... this time with a little more force. He finally woke up and tried to focus his eyes. He was staring at me as if he didn't know why I was so freaked out that he was here... IN MY BED!!

What the hell had I done with this man last night? Shit was so fuzzy, and my adrenaline was pumping like crazy. There was no way I was going to figure things out as long as he was here. He needed to get the hell out of my house. As I stood there watching him, I could feel my blood boiling to the point where it was about to overflow.

As he climbed out of the bed, he tried to have a conversation with me, but I wasn't interested. All I wanted was for him to leave. Whatever happened between us last night was going to stay there. After throwing him out of my house, I sat down on the side of the bed and tried to remember how I ended up with a stranger in my bed. My phone started ringing, so now I had to practically go on a scavenger hunt to find it.

I followed the ringing all the way to the foyer, where my purse rested on the table near the front door. I didn't know how my shit got there either. I opened the small clutch and pulled out my phone. I should've known it was Trinity calling.

Any other day, I'd ignore the call because I knew the first thing out of her mouth would be, "How are you? Are you alright?" I was even more fucked up now than I was yesterday when I found out that Charles had been fucking Jerry. However, I needed to speak with my best friend about what happened last night. Even though I couldn't remember shit!

"Hello," I answered.

"Nikola, thank God! I've been calling you all day yesterday and all night! Are you alright?"

I rolled my eyes because I knew she was going to ask me that.

"Trinity, I'm at home. How soon can you get here?"

"Consider me on my way," she said.

"Thanks girl."

"No thanks needed. Do you want me to pick up some coffee from Starbucks?"

"Yes please," I said.

"I'll be right over."

As soon as I ended the call with her, it started ringing again. I looked at the caller ID and saw that it was my mother calling. I knew darn well she didn't think I was going to answer the phone just to allow her to criticize me about what happened yesterday. I just let the phone go to voicemail and headed back to the bathroom to get dressed. As I rummaged through my closet, I couldn't help but think about Blaze. I didn't know why I was even thinking about him after what he did to me.

I wasn't sure what transpired between the two of us though, and that really had me feeling perplexed. Never in my life had I drunk as much as I had yesterday. I just wished I could remember how I ended up in bed with Blaze. All I knew was that I was walking funny, and had wonderful sensations transpiring in my vaginal region.

The thought that I had slept with a strange man last night made me feel a little dirty. That wasn't something that normally happened to me. I carried myself as a classy woman and spending the night with a stranger went against everything that I stood for. That shit was downright classless. I threw on a light pink sundress and slipped my feet in my comfortable house slippers before heading to the kitchen.

My phone started ringing again, so I checked to see who was calling. I rolled my eyes when I saw that it was Charles. What the hell did he want?

"What?" I answered in a voice laced with venom.

"Nikola are you okay?"

"How dare you ask me that after what you put me through on our wedding day!"

"I'm sorry that happened…"

"Sorry? YOU'RE SORRY?!!" I shouted.

"Look, I know that you're still upset with me, but I'd like the chance to come over there and talk to you for a bit."

"Charles, are you serious right now?"

"Yes, I need to make sure that you're okay," he said.

"You don't need to worry about me anymore. Go worry about Jerry's ass, and I mean it just the way I said it too," I said. "Emphasis on ASS!!"

"Can I at least come by and get the rest of my things?"

"What things? Oh, you mean the things I burned in the fire pit last night? Those things?"

Of course, I hadn't had a chance to do anything with Charles' things, but that's what I planned to do with them. Why should I give him anything after the way he treated me?

"Oh…"

"I never want to see or hear from you again, Charles. Do you understand?" I asked.

"Take care Nikola. No matter what happened, I really did lo…"

CLICK!!

No indeed honey. That bastard wasn't about to sit up there and tell me how much he loved me. Love wouldn't have made him cheat on me for the past nine months. Love would've had him behaving like a man getting married for the past nine months. And love wouldn't have had him bent over so Jerry could...

I ran to the toilet and threw up again. I didn't even have anything left in my system, but the thought of the man I was going to marry sleeping with another man literally made me sick. How could Charles have done that to me? How could he have done that to us?

"Fuck Charles!" I thought out loud as I flushed the toilet and went over to the sink to brush my teeth again. "That nigga doesn't deserve another thought coming from me."

DING DONG! DING DONG!

I wiped my mouth and went to answer the door. Seeing my best friend was exactly what I needed, and she had coffee and breakfast. "Girl, have you been crying again?"

"No," I responded.

"You look a little flustered, like you've been crying."

"No, Charles just called though."

"What the fuck did he want?"

"He said he was calling to check on me..."

"Wow! After what he did to you yesterday, what the hell does he think. I hope you told him to go back and jump on Jerry's dick!" she scoffed.

"Please stop it!" I laughed. "I just threw up thinking about that shit!"

"I'm just saying," she laughed. "That was some foul shit on his part! And for Jerry to make a scene like that at your wedding..."

"I know, but I'm glad he did it before we said I do. What if Charles and I would've gotten married and was still sleeping with Jerry? Like, what if I would've gotten pregnant?"

"Girl, count your lucky stars that shit didn't happen!"

"I know right."

We sat down at the dining room table. I grabbed a cup of coffee as she dug into the IHOP bag. She handed me a plate which contained a bacon omelet with an order of hash browns. I was grateful for my friend because I hadn't eaten anything since yesterday morning. That's why the alcohol had hit me as hard as it did last night.

"So, how are you feeling?" Trinity asked as she sat down across from to me. "Be completely honest with me."

"Well, if I had to speak from my experience yesterday, I'd have to say I feel like shit. But I'm going to speak from what I woke up to this morning and say I'm confused..."

"What happened this morning? Why are you feeling confused?"

"To be honest BFF, the past 24 hours has been one big blur."

"So, now I'm confused," she said as she stared at me.

"I know. This whole thing is quite confusing. Okay, I remember running out of the hotel following that disastrous almost wedding. I'm very clear about that," I said as I took a bite of my food. "But after I left the wedding, I hopped in the limo and asked the driver to drive around. I ended up at a blues club in the French Quarter."

"Really? So, you went out to celebrate?"

"No, I mean, not really. I had a few drinks... hell, more than a few drinks. Girl, I was LIT!!"

"Damn! Now you know you can't hold your liquor," Trinity said.

"I know. I tried to pace myself, but that didn't work. I think I even fell asleep at one point..."

"Fell asleep? In the club?"

"Girl yes! That's what I'm trying to tell you. I was fucked all the way up!" I admitted.

"Tell me something... if you were so fucked up, how did you get home?"

"That's the confusing part. I'm not sure how I got home, but I think this dude from the bar brought me home..."

"Was he cute?"

"What?" I asked.

"Was he cute?" she repeated.

"He was cute, but that ain't what confused me," I said.

"Girl, you are going in circles and confusing me. Just get to the point!"

"Well, I think we can both admit that yesterday wasn't my day Trinity. Nothing that I did was like me, at all. I mean, can you believe that Charles and Jerry have been fucking around on me? I'm still having trouble coming to terms with that shit," I said.

"I'm so sorry that happened to you sis. You didn't deserve that at all. I never would've thought..."

"Me either. That's what shocked me the most, but the more time I had to think about it, the more it started to make sense."

"MAKE SENSE?! How the hell you make sense out of that bullshit?" Trinity asked.

"Well, to be honest, Charles and I hadn't had sex in months..."

"What? Y'all ain't had sex in months?"

"Nope."

"Not even oral?"

"Nope, nothing."

"And you were okay with that?"

"I wouldn't say that I was okay with it. I guess because I was working and planning the wedding, I didn't make a big deal about it."

"Whew chile! Lemme tell you something, if me and Jason miss more than two nights without having sex, it's gonna be a problem. I wanna know who, what, when, where and how because if he ain't giving it to me, he's got to be dipping it somewhere else!"

"I just hadn't really thought about it though. I mean, planning the wedding was a lot of work..."

"I know. Who do you think helped you?" she asked as she side eyed me.

"So, you should understand. Not only was it a lot of work, but it was also stressful," I said. I was really making excuses for the lack of sex that Charles and I were having at the time. I guess I just never thought he'd cheat on me. I never thought he'd betray me like that, especially after I revealed what happened between me and Miles.

"Well, for future reference, never let your man get away with not giving you no dick for six months again! If that would've happened to me, I would've called the wedding off and kicked his fucking ass!" Trinity said.

"I guess I hadn't thought about it."

"Shit, it's all I think about!"

"Look at me Trinity," I said.

"Oh, no! Don't you start doubting yourself again just because of Charles' nasty ass!"

"What's wrong with me?" I asked as a huge lump formed in my throat. I just couldn't believe another man had cheated on me except this time it was with a man. Wasn't I good enough to have a husband?

"Not a damn thing is wrong with you, so you can just get that out of your head right now!"

"Well, something must be wrong with me for these men to cheat on me!"

"Nothing is wrong with you Nikki! Something is wrong with them!" Trinity said. "Shit, Miles was just a jerk and I told you that from the beginning! And Charles is GAY! Him being a fruitcake has nothing to do with you! He was being deceitful about his 'locked in the closet' status the whole time! His sexual crisis has nothing to do with you!"

I was hearing the words, but they weren't processing. All I could think about was how played I felt at the altar yesterday. "Girl, Charles wanted to do the muddy booty dance! Were you going to allow him to leave tire and skid marks in your ass?!"

What the hell was Trinity talking about? Of course, I wasn't going to let him fuck me in the ass! Was she crazy?

"Girl bye! There's no way..."

"Exactly! Besides, he didn't want a woman's ass... he wanted a man's! Nothing is wrong with you sis. Shit was wrong with him!" she said. "Whatchu need to do is sue him for the money you spent on that wedding! Shit, Jerry too since he wanted to stand up and sing that shit like a bird, get his ass too!"

"Nah, suing them would only cause further embarrassment for me. I couldn't do that..."

"Bullshit! You're embarrassed because your wedding didn't go as planned. Charles should be embarrassed because a secret he was trying to keep came out... in front of everybody!"

"Did I tell you he called and asked if he could come by for his clothes and stuff?"

"The nerve! What'd you tell him?"

"I lied and said I had burned them in the fire pit out back." I said, feeling ashamed for lying to that man.

"Well, let's not leave it a lie any longer."

"Whaddya mean?"

"I mean, let's get all his shit and burn it!" Trinity said with a huge smile on her face.

"I can't do that..."

"Shit, the hell you can't, and I'll help you!"

She jumped up and practically flew to my bedroom to get Charles' things. "TRINITY!" I called as she started to gather his toiletries and things that he had at my house. "You can't just burn his things!"

"This is your house, so technically these are your things. You don't want them anymore, so we're gonna take them out back and burn them!" she said as she headed for the back door.

"TRINITY!!" I called as I followed her. "We can't..."

"Look sis, you already told him that's what you did to his things! That means, you had it on your mind. I say do it... I promise it'll make you feel ten times better."

"I can't do that... can I?"

"Yes, you can. He owes it to you so you can feel good." She tossed the clothes and items in the pit. She sprayed lighter fluid on top of the stuff as I gawked in shock. She handed me the box of matches and smiled. "Do it!"

As I took the matches from her and looked at the stuff saturated in fluid, I thought, *Why not? I mean, he can't use them anyway because they're soaked in lighter fluid.*

I flicked the match against the box and watched the fire attach itself to the little stick. Without another thought, I tossed it on top of Charles' things. There was a loud crackle as his things went up in flames.

"YAAASSSS!!" Trinity shouted as she clapped her hands in celebratory fashion. She took off for the inside of the house.

"Where are you going?" I asked.

"To get the rest of his shit!"

I wanted to stop her, but I didn't because she was right... it did feel good to watch his shit go up in smoke. That's what he deserved after what he did to me yesterday.

Chapter four

Trinity

I had been trying to reach Nikola ever since she ran out yesterday. I couldn't believe things had played out the way that they did. After she left, Charles kept trying to talk to me to get me to get her to understand. Let me take y'all back to that time when I was ready to bust him and her mom in the head...

So, Nikola ran out leaving me to deal with the riff raff, her mom and Charles. I couldn't stand either one of them right now, but I was going to try my best to keep my feelings in check.

"*Trinity you have to talk to Nikola for me!*" Charles begged as I stared at him in disgust.

"*Why are you even still here Charles? The wedding was called off and the guests are leaving. Why don't you go get your little boyfriend and get on somewhere?*" I asked.

"*I need you to talk to Nikola for me... please!*"

"*And say what? What the hell do you expect me to say to my best friend after this?*"

"I don't know..." He looked as if he was ready to cry, but I didn't care. My heart was already breaking for what Nikola was going through.

"Charles, why did you do that to her? Answer me that question..."

"I don't know. I never meant for that to happen. I'M NOT EVEN GAY!!"

"The hell you ain't!" Ms. Rose came up behind us. As much as I didn't like that little woman, maybe she could get Charles to get the hell outta here.

"Ms. Rose please, I am really not in the mood," Charles said.

"I don't give a fuck what you're in the mood for! Why the hell didn't you tell my daughter that you were gay? Why would you let her think y'all were getting married if you was taking it up the ass?" Ms. Rose asked.

"Ms. Rose please, this doesn't concern you!" Charles said in an agitated tone.

"That's my daughter who just ran out of here and you trying to tell me that you breaking her heart doesn't concern me? I oughta slap the black off yo ass!"

That lil woman was too damn feisty for her age. She was always in other people's business, which usually bothered me. Right now, I didn't give a shit about Charles or what he wanted to say.

"WHY DIDN'T YOU TELL NIKOLA THAT YOU WERE GAY?!!" she yelled.

"I'M NOT GAY!!" Charles yelled. "What part of that don't you people understand?"

"Oh, I'm sorry, but maybe we're having a hard time understanding it because we don't know any straight men who bends over for other men!" I said.

"I sho' don't know no men like that... not no straight ones," Ms. Rose said. "But you keep telling yourself that you aren't gay. Maybe one day, your dick will believe that shit."

"Look Charles, how you live your lifestyle and who you choose to be with is your business. But today was supposed to be my best friend's wedding day. She has been planning this day ever since you popped the question. So, forgive me if I don't feel any empathy towards you and a situation that you created. My concern right now is for my best friend and making sure that she's okay," I said as I pulled out my phone and called Nikola.

The phone rang until it went to voicemail. As I made my way to the door, Charles called after me. "Trinity!"

I turned to face him as I ended yet another unanswered call to Nikola. "What?" I asked through clenched teeth.

"Can you please tell her that I'm sorry? I never meant for this to happen and I love her," he said through tear filled eyes.

"I can tell her the sorry part when I see her, but that other stuff... I can't. I don't believe that you love her. Otherwise, you wouldn't have hurt her," I said as I exited the room.

I made my way down the stairs as Jerry made his way upstairs. Lord have mercy, I thought. The two of them in the same room with Nikola's mom... it was about to go down. However, I couldn't concern myself with that. I had to go down to the reception hall to inform the caterers that the wedding was off. Imagine my surprise when I entered and found that the guests were dancing and eating.

"Wow!" That was all I could muster as I watched them acting like the wedding had happened. Well, I guess I may as well join them because I was hungry and there was no way this good food was about to go to waste.

I found Jason talking to the other groomsmen. The two of us headed to the buffet and got our plates filled. Then we sat and ate. We danced and even cut the wedding cake. I hated that this had happened to Nikola, but I was glad that the truth came out before the wedding. It would have been ten times worse if she had found out the after they were married.

I headed back inside Nikola's house to get some more of Charles' things while Nikola stayed outside to watch over the fire. Shit, after the way he did her yesterday, I was more than happy to help her get over that bastard. Any man that would string a woman along for nine months while he fucked another man is an asshole. He not only deceived Nikki, but he let her keep spending her money on wedding plans. He knew he wasn't going to go through with that wedding, and if he didn't know when she was planning, he definitely knew when he saw Jerry in attendance.

The fact that he stood at the altar with Nikki while Jerry sat with the other guests made me wonder what he thought was going to happen. Like did he think they would get married and Jerry would come over and congratulate them? That shit was a ticking time bomb ready to go off and he should've done the right thing. I ran back outside with some more of his shit and handed them to Nikola. She needed to be the one to throw the clothes in the fire. She was the one struggling to make peace with what happened, so she was going to be the one who needed to feel the relief.

She smiled as she tossed his things in the fire. "How do you feel?" I asked.

"I feel great!" she said with a smile as she tossed his pants in the pit.

"Well, you keep doing that and I'll be right back."

"Where are you going now?"

"I'm going to get a bottle of wine and two glasses! It's time to celebrate!"

"A bottle of wine at this time of the day?"

"Hey, it's five o'clock somewhere!" I said as I headed inside.

I knew that Nikki was most likely feeling a little apprehensive about drinking, especially since she had drunk so heavily yesterday. But hey, that was a thing of the past. Today was a new day and we were going to treat it as such. She no longer had to worry about Charles' ass, so she was free to do what she wanted to do. Besides, I had a feeling Ms. Rose was going to pay her a visit today, so she was going to need some alcohol in her system to deal with her mom.

I came across a bottle of Moscato, grabbed two wine glasses and headed back out. By that time, she was done burning Charles' clothes and was sitting in the chair watching the fire. I walked out and handed her a glass before uncorking the wine bottle.

As I relaxed in the chair next to her, I asked, "So, how do you feel now?"

"Great! I feel as if a weight has been lifted off my shoulders. Thanks for coming over," she said with a smile.

"You don't need to thank me. We're sisters and that's what sisters do. Besides, you would've done the same thing for me."

"You got that right!" The two of us lifted and clinked our glasses together. We sat quietly for a few minutes and I could sense that something was on her mind. However, I didn't want to push her about it because she'd tell me when she was ready. "Ummm, I think I had sex last night," she quietly admitted.

"Well damn! Was it with the cutie who brought you home last night?" I asked.

"Yea."

"You go girl! The quickest way to get over that loser is to jump on someone else!"

"I'm not jumping on someone else!"

"A one-night stand... even better! Either way, it got your mind off Charles. So, tell me what happened? What's his name? Where's he from?" I asked.

"His name is Blaze but that's all I know."

"So, he left without speaking to you this morning?" I asked. "Because if that's what he did, I need to go find his ass and beat him down!"

"No, that's not exactly how that happened."

"Well, what happened?"

"Look, I woke up butt naked in my bed next to a naked stranger, so I did what any woman in her right mind would do..."

"Which is?"

"I threw his ass out of my house!" she said.

I knew she was serious and seemed a little upset too, but this whole thing was comical to me. As serious in the face as she was, I was cracking up with laughter. "What's funny Trinity?"

"What's funny is that I could actually see your facial expressions when you threw him out! I mean, he probably thought he was about to get some more nookie this morning. Instead of that, you threw him out! That's some funny shit!"

"Okay, I'll admit it is a little funny," she said as she giggled a little.

"I'm tryna tell you!"

The two of us had a good laugh about her little indiscretion last night. I didn't talk about it that much because I sensed she was going through some issues with that. Nikola wasn't the type of woman to have a one-night stand, so I was sure she was feeling some kind of way about it.

When I left her house a little after four that afternoon, she was in much better spirits. I was glad that I was able to help her get out of her funk and realize that nothing that happened with Miles or Charles was her fault. Yes, me and Jason hooked her up with Miles because I thought he was a cool dude. I mean, he and Jason had been working together for years and Jason would always have funny stuff to tell me about something Miles did.

So, I thought it would be a good idea to play matchmaker for him and Nikki. The two of them dated for several months without any incidents. When Miles asked Nikki to marry him, I was just as thrilled as she was. I couldn't be happier for my friend.

Let me tell y'all a little something about my best friend Nikki. She is such a strong person and she has been through so much. She's always been a thick and round chick, even when she was a little girl. Kids would often tease and bully Nikki because of her size. I had to step in several times to intervene because I couldn't take how those kids could be so cruel.

She and I weren't even friends at that time, but we quickly bonded and had been glued at the hips ever since. I didn't even think she'd want to be friends with me when I first approached her because while she was thick, I was thin like my dad's side of the family. She had chubby cheeks and I had high cheekbones like a top model. She had big arms, while I had toned arms. But regardless of how opposite we were, I was still going to step in and save her from those who couldn't appreciate her big beautiful self.

Sometimes, I felt horrible for Nikki. Like, when I had dates and she didn't, it broke my heart. While I had a date for prom, Nikki went alone. We still hung out together though, but I knew she felt like a third wheel. Her mom didn't make things any better.

Ms. Rose was always calling Nikki names because of her size. I think it's horrible when your own parent belittles you. I mean, if your own mother won't stick up for you, how is that supposed to make you feel? Nikki's mom always called her fat, funky, Moby dickish, Shamu, Flipper, just all kinds of foul names. Why not get Nikki on the right track to help her lose weight instead of making her feel like she should be ashamed of who she is?

It took me a long time to convince my bestie that she was just as beautiful as anyone else. Just because she packed on a few more pounds than some, didn't make her any less attractive. Nikki had a big, round, beautiful face. No one could take that away from her. I showed her how to apply makeup to enhance her beauty. I showed her how to shop for clothes that hugged her curves in a positive way instead of wearing those tent-like dresses and shirts that made her look bigger than she actually was.

Nikki was a very beautiful 25-year old woman. She was just voluptuous and thick. But she had an amazing personality and any man would be lucky to call her his wife. She just needed to keep the negative people out of her life and fill her space with positivity. Ms. Rose was one of those negative people who needed to stay as far away from Nikki as possible. She was the biggest critic of her own child and the biggest thorn in my side.

Thank God Nikki took my advice and learned to love herself for who she was. A person couldn't find love from anyone else if they didn't love their own self. It was hard to teach her because her mom had done a wonderful job convincing her that she'd never find love. Ms. Rose always told her that no man would want a woman who could out eat him at a buffet. I'm telling you... that woman was something else, and I didn't mean that in a good way.

Nikki would be fine as long as she kept her mom away from her. She didn't need that little woman raining on her already damp parade.

Chapter five

Charles

I never thought that Jerry would do that shit. When I spoke to him last night, I begged him not to attend the wedding. I knew that he was feeling some kind of way about me going through with the marriage to Nikola. I was so confused, and I knew that he was too. I had been living a double life for the past nine months and I planned to continue living it as long as possible. You see, the company I worked for had a morals clause which I signed when I started with the company. In my eyes, sleeping with another man would definitely go against any morals of the company.

I couldn't afford to lose my job, especially one that paid me $125,000 a year. I was one of the top executives for the company. All the other executives were happily married with kids. After every meeting, I'd get asked the same question... when was I going to get married? So, I went out and found a bride, Nikola.

She was beautiful, but man was she big. I had come to love Nikola, but I wasn't in love with her. How could I be when I was trapped in a closet and lusting for men? I hated that I couldn't love a woman like other men. I wanted to be normal, and this shit that I was feeling definitely wasn't normal. I had been hiding the real me from everyone who thought they knew me for as long as I could remember. Lying was something I had gotten so used to doing that it felt like the truth. I almost believed that I could be happy with Nikola.

Jerry made me believe that he'd keep our secret and we'd continue to see each other even after I got married. But he lied. He switched the whole game up on me. When we spoke the night before, he swore to keep this just between us. He knew how important my job was to me and that it took me years to get where I was in the company. I thought his job meant a lot to him also, but obviously, I was wrong.

Jerry came out and told everyone in my family, Nikola's family and some of our coworkers that I was gay. How could he do that to me? How could he ruin my life and career that way? Not only that, but he ruined his own career because fraternizing within the company was strictly prohibited. Now, we would both be without a job come Monday.

I flew up the stairs to try and get Nikola to listen to me, but she wasn't having it. She wouldn't even look at me. She just ran out. I tried to speak with Trinity so she could talk to Nikola for me. If I could just convince her that this was just a misunderstanding, maybe she would marry me, and the senior executives would think that Jerry was just kidding. That would be a longshot though.

Dammit! He had literally ruined everything.

After Nikola and Trinity ran out, I was left with Ms. Rose. I wished she had left with Trinity because I wasn't in the mood for her shit right now. Before she could say anything, in walked Jerry. Just great! Now, she was about to give us the business.

"Well, I should've known your little boyfriend was gonna come and check on you!" She said as she crossed her arms over her chest while staring both of us down.

"Look lady, I don't know you from a can of paint..."

"Look twinkle toes," she interrupted Jerry. "You ain't gotta know me! What you and this bitch did was ruin my daughter's wedding day! You two ought to be ashamed of yourselves because you both knew that you were gay nine months ago and continued with this charade!"

"First of all, twinkle toes ain't my name boo! And second of all, I wanted to tell Nikola the truth way before today, but Charles didn't want to!" Jerry said pointing the finger at me.

Now, Ms. Rose was back to glaring at me. "So, you could've prevented this shit from happening the way that it did..."

"Yes, but..."

"But nothing! Why would you purposely embarrass my child that way? Didn't you even consider how this shit would make her feel?" Ms. Rose asked.

"Um, from what I understand, you don't give two farts about Nikola. Don't be jumping down Charles' back like you're some saint of a mother..."

WHAP!

My mouth hit the floor when Ms. Rose slapped Jerry. I should've known it was coming because he was out of line with the disrespect. Shit that he and I spoke about was supposed to be kept between us. Yet, there he was blabbing it which got him smacked.

Ms. Rose pointed her finger in his face and said, "Don't you ever speak about my feelings for my daughter! You don't know shit about me or her!" Then she turned to me. "I know whatever he's saying came from your pussy ass mouth."

"Lady, you are lucky I ain't trying to fuck up my Gucci fit! Otherwise..."

"Otherwise what twinkle toes?" Ms. Rose asked.

I had to step in between the two of them to keep them from going at it. "Let's just get out of here!" I told Jerry.

"Y'all better get!" Ms. Rose said.

We left and headed down the stairs. I couldn't believe this shit had even happened to me. Today was supposed to be my wedding day and Jerry had fucked everything up. Why would he do this when he knew it could cost me my job?

The next day, I woke up feeling worse than the day before. I couldn't believe that I had hurt Nikola that way. I knew that messing with Jerry was wrong, but I couldn't help myself. I guess I never thought that he would betray my secret. I certainly didn't think that he would do it on my wedding day. When I woke up, by myself mind you, I headed straight to the bathroom to take a shower. Jerry wanted to spend the night with me, but I refused.

He was upset because he couldn't understand why we couldn't be together, especially now that everything was out in the open. I was even more upset with him for talking about our business. I decided to call Nikola just to see if she'd be willing to hear me out. She wasn't. I even asked if I could come by and get my things that I had at her place and she informed me that she had burned them in the fire pit.

I couldn't believe she would go that far, but I also couldn't blame her for being so upset. Jerry had dropped a bombshell on her, and he had done it in the worst way. I had no idea how I could make it up to Nikola. I didn't even know if I'd ever be able to make that up to her. I had ruined one of the best days of her life.

Dammit! Why hadn't I seen Jerry seated with the guests before the wedding started? I could've spoken to him beforehand and made sure his head was on straight. Jerry was ringing my phone off the hook, but I didn't want to speak to him right now. I needed to speak to Nikola. I needed to see her and apologize to her.

I made my way to the bedroom to get dressed. It was almost 4:30 in the afternoon. Maybe she'd be willing to listen to me now that she had some time to cool off. I took a shower and brushed my teeth. I threw on a pair of grey sweatpants and a black t-shirt. I pulled on some Polo socks and put on my black Air Forces before grabbing my keys and heading out. By the time I got to Nikola's place, it was almost 5:15.

I knocked on the door, hoping that she'd let me in so we could talk.

Chapter six

Nikola

Trinity was just what the doctor ordered for me to feel better about everything. She was such a character that I couldn't stay upset for long. She helped me see that what happened wasn't my fault, it was Charles' fault. Burning Charles' things also helped me feel good. The thought had crossed my mind which was why I mentioned it to him, but I never would've gone through with it if it hadn't been for Trinity egging me on. She was the definition of a true friend, even though she and I were total opposites.

Trinity always had the courage to stand up for herself and others. I had to learn to be as sharp as she was. Growing up with just my mom belittling and ridiculing me always made me feel inadequate and lack confidence. I had no self-esteem or self-worth, nothing. Trinity was my rock and I'd forever be grateful to her for being there for me when I needed her most.

After she left, I continued to sip wine while watching the smoldering embers of the fire. I had quite a few glasses of wine... Trinity and I had emptied the bottle out. Of course, I drank more than she did because she had to drive home.

DING DONG! DING DONG! DING DONG!

I rolled my eyes upward and went inside to answer the door. I didn't know who it was but thought it might be Trinity coming back. I put the empty wine bottle on the bar and pulled the door back. I almost dropped my glass of wine when I saw Charles standing on my doorstep.

"Nope! Not today!" I said as I tried to shut the door in his face.

"Please Nikki..."

"Don't you ever fucking call me that! Nikki is the name my friends and family call me. You are neither my friend nor a member of my family! My name is Nikola!"

"I'm sorry. Can I please talk to you? I promise I won't stay long," he said.

"Oh, I know you won't. I don't know what the hell you're doing here, but you have five minutes to say what you need to say and get the hell out!"

"Thanks, I appreciate you hearing me out..."

"Four minutes," I said as I held up four fingers.

"I never meant for any of that to happen yesterday. Just know that when I said I love you, I meant that. I wanted to marry you. I still want to marry you..."

"Okay, times up!" I said.

There was no way that I was going to listen to that man utter another lie to me.

"You said five minutes," he said looking confused.

"Yea, well, I changed my mind. I won't listen to you lie to me."

"I'm not lying Nikola! I really care about you."

"If that were true, you wouldn't have a nigga's dick stuffed up your ass!"

"Don't say that," he said sadly.

"Don't say what? The truth?" I asked. I was definitely confused by his words. "Oh yea, I forgot that Jerry said you were still in denial."

"I'm not in denial..."

"LIAR!! If you are allowing a nigga to fuck you in the ass or vice versa, that makes you GAY!! YOU ARE GAY AS FUCK!!" I yelled. I didn't know if he was in denial or not, but if he was, I was about to let him know what it was.

"Nikola, I'm not gay! You and I were sleeping together..."

"Boy bye! We ain't had sex in over six months, and that's because you was getting it from someone else. I never even allowed myself to believe that you were cheating on me. I never would've thought that about you. I just assumed that you were giving me my space because you knew that the wedding planning was stressing me out. In reality, you were just fucking around with someone else!"

"It wasn't like that..."

"You know what? I don't even give a fuck what it was like! I am not going to give you another chance to make me cry. I want you to get the hell out of my house!" I said as I walked toward the door.

"Nikola please, we can still get married!" Charles said.

"I know you lying! After what I found out yesterday, I wouldn't marry you if you were the last man on this damn earth! Now, get the hell out of my house Charles!"

He looked at me like he had something else to say, but then he looked at my face and thought better of it. He stepped outside and I eyed him down. "You really had me fooled. But now that I know the truth about you, don't you ever bring your ass around here again!"

I slammed the door in his face and headed to the bedroom. This wine was making me sleepy. I fell in bed and shut my eyes immediately.

I don't know how long I was asleep when I started having these weird dreams. It was about me and Blaze. We were in my bed and he was doing some things to me that would make an old lady blush. Blaze had lifted my leg on his shoulder and was deep inside me. He was penetrating me, and I was loving it. He kissed me and I kissed him back. I had never been kissed like that before, not by Miles and certainly not by Charles.

The crazy thing about this dream was that it seemed so real. I never had experienced something so real before in my life. It was almost as if it had happened. The kisses were so soft and sensual, passionate and longing. I woke up the next morning with very wet panties and a huge wet spot in my bed. It felt as if my lips were searing hot, like if they had gotten pressed by a waffle iron or something.

I slid out of bed and rushed to take a shower... a cold one. Lord knows I needed one after the restless night I had. I slipped in the shower and let the cool water rain on my hot pocket. I still couldn't believe that I had dreamed about Blaze last night. Just the thought of his hands all over me made me cringe. I wasn't into thugs. I didn't care what businesses he owned. At the end of the day, he was still a thug in my eyes.

Once I finished bathing, I stepped out of the shower and grabbed a towel to dry off with. I wasn't completely dry as I reached for the scented lotion on the counter. I applied lotion to my already damp skin so it would make the scent last longer. I inhaled the blueberry custard lotion before putting the bottle back on the countertop. I brushed my teeth and washed my face. I really had to get that man out of my head.

My phone started ringing so I rushed to answer it. I hoped it was Trinity because I wanted to talk to her about that dream, but as soon as I looked at the caller ID my hope dissipated. It was my mother and she was the last person I wanted to speak with feeling how I was at the moment. I let it go to voicemail just like the last 25 calls she made. Just in case y'all haven't figured it out yet, my mother and I didn't really have the best relationship.

She sent me a text message...

Mom: You need to pick up that phone Nikola! I ain't gon' keep playing with you like that! If you don't answer, I'm coming over there

I rolled my eyes because I knew she wasn't about to drive an hour to come over to my place. I distanced myself like that purposely because I knew she wouldn't want to keep driving that far to come visit with me. However, her next text shocked the shit out of me and forced me to pick up the phone.

Mom: I ain't playing either b/c I'm right around the corner from yo house at the hotel

Dammit! My phone started ringing two minutes after I read the last text.

"Hello mother," I said.

"Don't you hello mother me young lady? Why haven't you been picking up the damn phone? I've only been trying to check up on you after that bullshit wedding flopped yesterday!"

"And this is the reason why I wasn't answering you. I knew you were going to talk shit about what happened the day before yesterday."

"Don't you take that tone with me!"

"Mom I'm a grown ass woman and as long as I'm not being disrespectful towards you, I should be able to speak how I want to in my own home!" I said.

"Keep talking to me like that and you'll see..."

"Why are you calling me?"

"Didn't I just tell you that I wanted to check on you? How are you holding up?"

"I'm fine. I'm just trying to put what happened behind me and move on with my life!" I said. "When are you going back home?"

"I'm about to check out of this hotel and head back home now. I gotta work tomorrow, unlike some people," she said sarcastically.

"The only reason I'm off this week is because I was supposed to be on my honeymoon. So, don't say it like I'm off vacationing or something," I said.

"That's exactly what you need to be doing. You need to go on a vacation to the Bahamas or someplace beautiful like that. Somewhere you can go fuck a

Bahamian or Dominican and forget all about that gay bird you almost said I do to…"

"Mom, please…"

"No Nikki, listen to me. You were dumped at the altar by a man who was getting his asshole ripped open by some other dude. You're probably thinking that shit was your fault. That it was something you didn't do enough of. I'm sure you're sitting over there wondering if you sucked his dick enough, or if he cheated because your ass was too fat! I done told you that you needed to lose some damn weight before you end up on *My 600 pound Life* on TLC."

"Wow! Really mom? If this is supposed to make me feel better…"

"I'm just trying to get you to see that you need to go lay on a beach somewhere. Well, maybe a beach isn't the place for someone your size. They might mistake you for a beached whale or something…"

This was the shit I hated about my mom. Mothers were supposed to make their daughters feel special and good about themselves. My mom never did that for me. She always made me feel horrible about myself, my weight, just everything. Why couldn't she say something positive to make me feel good because of what I went through? What kind of mother beat up their daughter's self-esteem that way and considered it helping?

"You hear what I'm saying to you Nikki? Go fuck a Jamaican or Dominican man out of the country. And don't say you can't do it because you're too fat. Those men love fucking American women and they will jump on your big ass in a heartbeat. Shit, it might take two of them to satisfy your big ass appetite, but I know..."

CLICK!!

I knew it was disrespectful to hang up on a parent, but I wasn't going to listen to her shit for one more minute. If I wouldn't have ended that call, I would've definitely been disrespectful in the worst way. She would've surely felt my wrath if I hadn't hung up on her. She called like four more times, but I didn't answer. I couldn't take her anymore. Why couldn't I just have a normal fucking mother like Trinity or other kids did? Why did I have to have her as my mom?

The next four nights were pretty restless for me. I kept dreaming about Blaze to the point where I had to go down to the blues club. The only reason I went there was because I felt the need to apologize. Apparently, my dreams weren't really just dreams or at least they didn't seem that way. They seemed to be actual scenes that had taken place the night of the wedding. I mean, I kept having the exact same dream, frame for frame, scene for scene.

I decided to confront Blaze about what really happened that night. He had tried to explain what happened that morning, but I wouldn't listen. I guess I was going to have to listen this time if I wanted to know what had transpired between us. So, I got all dressed up and sprayed some Dolce & Gabana Light Blue perfume, grabbed my keys and headed out the door.

I really didn't know what I'd say to him when I saw him. He might never wanna speak to me again, but at least I tried. I slid into the driver's seat of my 2018 Chevy Impala and clicked my seatbelt in place. The drive to the bar took only 20 minutes. Once I parked my car, I became a little nervous.

"Maybe this isn't a good idea," I said out loud to myself. "Maybe I didn't need to ask him anything. I mean, we both woke up naked in my bed. My thighs were hurting, so it was pretty apparent what had gone down that night."

Ugh! The struggle was real.

I took a deep breath, got out the car and went inside. As my eyes roamed the club, I tried to see if I could spot Blaze. I didn't see him, so I headed to the bar. I sat down and waited to be helped by the bartender. I recognized him as the same guy who served me that Saturday.

"Hello, what can I get you?" he asked.

"Um, is Blaze here?" I asked shyly.

"No, he won't be in until tomorrow night."

"Oh."

"Would you like me to tell him that you stopped by?"

"No, that's okay," I said as I slid off the barstool.

"Are you sure?"

"Yea."

I walked out the door and headed back home. I should've stayed to listen to the live band, especially since I had gotten all dressed up. I just didn't feel like staying anymore. I had come to the club for answers from the only person who could give them to me, but he wasn't here. The bartender said he'd be there tomorrow night, so I guess I'd come back then.

The next night, I got dressed up again and made my way to the club around ten. I walked in and headed to the bar. I ordered a Shirley Temple and asked for Blaze. The bartender pointed him out sitting at a table in a dimly lit corner. I took a deep breath and made my way over there.

"Hi," I greeted with a flimsy smile.

"Hey."

"May I join you?"

"Sure," he said as he studied my face.

"You do remember me, don't you?" I asked shyly. I knew damn well he remembered me. How the hell could he forget my big ass body?

"Yes, I never forget a pretty face. You're the beautiful bride that threw me out yo crib last weekend," he answered with a smile.

"I'm sorry about that. I mean, please understand my position. I was really drunk the night before. I didn't even remember how I got home, so to see you in my bed... it was just a bit much."

"I'm not trippin' beautiful. I can understand how you would feel that way, but I can promise you that I wouldn't have stayed if you hadn't asked me to."

"That's kinda what I wanted to talk to you about. How did you end up staying the night?"

"I drove you home because I felt responsible for you. I mean, this is my spot. I'd hate for something to happen to you after you left here knowing that you were tipsy, ya know?"

"I was drunk, not just tipsy!"

"Well, inebriated for sure."

Wow! Such a big word for a thug, I thought.

"Yea, definitely that."

"Anyway, I planned to just drop you off. So, after getting your address from you, you fell asleep on the drive there. So, I unlocked your door with a key I found in your purse. Then I scooped you up and brought you inside..."

"Scooped me up? What you mean you scooped me up?"

"I mean, I picked you up and carried you inside your place. I found your bedroom and placed you on the bed. Then you asked me to help you remove your dress and shoes. Which I did. Then I told you I was going to leave you and that's when you asked me not to leave you."

"Really?" I asked, finding it hard to believe that I wouldn't want a stranger to leave me... in my own damn house.

"Yea. You said you didn't want to be rejected by another man again today. I felt really bad for you Nikola."

He remembered my name! I couldn't believe he remembered my name! Wow!

"So, then what happened?"

"Well, I told you I'd stay with you, but only planned to stay long enough for you to fall asleep, then I'd be out. But when you walked out of the bathroom with that robe on and nothing underneath... at the end of the day, I'm a man before anything," he said.

"So, you're admitting that you took advantage of me?"

"No, I'm not saying that at all. What I'm saying is that with you being naked and throwing yourself at me, I just lost that battle to be a gentleman."

"Throwing myself at you?"

"Well, you came out of the bathroom without any clothes and then you kissed me. What was I supposed to do?" he asked.

"You could've walked away. You knew that I was drunk," I said.

"I knew that you were drunk, but you were also naked and begging me not to leave you. Look, I'm sorry if you think I took advantage of you because that wasn't my intent. I just wanted to make sure you got home safely."

"I bet you did..."

"I did! I don't know what kind of man you think I am, but I can assure you I'm not the type of man to take pussy from a woman unless she's offering it to me."

"But you did!"

"No, I didn't! I'm not that kind of dude!"

"I know your type. You're a thug and y'all always take and do what the hell y'all want!"

"Wow! Look lady," he said as he stood up from his seat. "I'm sorry things got out of hand that night. You were under the influence and I wasn't, so I should've used my better judgment. But what you're implying... nah, I'm not that type of dude. And I may have done some shady shit in the past, but nothing like what you're suggesting. I don't know what else it you'd like me to say to prove to you how sorry I am."

With that, he walked away from my table. Well, that certainly didn't go as planned. He seemed like a nice guy, but something about that night just didn't seem right to me. How dare he sleep with me when he knew the condition I was in! How dare he fuck me when he knew the state of mind that I was in! And for him to just walk away like this shit was over... aw hell naw!!

This shit was just getting started...

Chapter seven

Blaze

Okay, I could admit that I probably shouldn't have gone all the way with Nikola that night, but she begged me for it. How the hell was I supposed to just walk away from all that? I mean, she came out of the bathroom butt ass naked. I didn't undress her, she undressed herself. I had a feeling she would react some kind of way when she awoke and saw me in her bed, but I didn't think it would be like that. Surely, she had to remember something about that night to let her know that what we did was consensual, and she wanted it too.

After I hightailed it outta there, I hopped in my truck and headed home. I hadn't seen or heard from ol' girl until she walked over to my table tonight. I thought after she had time to cool off, she'd come to realize that things didn't happen the way that she thought they did. However, it seemed as if she was still holding a grudge and blaming me for everything that had happened. I wasn't sure what she was insinuating, but I wished I had never slept with her ass.

I knew that I was wrong for giving her the business, but she practically begged me for it. When she stepped out of that bathroom without anything under that robe, she should've known what was about to go down. I'm a damn man and I'm a respectable man. I guess what I should've done was walked away from the pussy, no matter how much she was trying to give it to me. I could admit that I was dead wrong for taking it when I knew that she was a little tipsy.

She said she was drunk, and she might have been when we walked out of the club. But she definitely wasn't drunk when she walked out of that bathroom. Nah, she was fully aware of everything she was doing when she came on to me. In our conversation a few seconds ago, it almost felt as if she was accusing me of something. And that something was a pretty serious accusation, so I wasn't going to sit and listen to that shit.

She had nerve to call me a thug and tell me that she knew my type. What the fuck was my type? She knew nothing about me at all. Had she known my type, she'd know that while I had done some questionable shit in my past, I was a changed man. I had worked hard to put that life behind me. I was a totally different man from who I was back then. Back then, I didn't give a fuck who

I hurt or what I did to get what I wanted and that shit almost cost me my damn life.

Back then, I was the man and I ran shit. I used to be one of the biggest drug dealers in the state of Texas not too long ago. When I say one of the biggest, that's exactly what I meant. I had so many soldiers working for me you would swear that I was a lieutenant in the army. I practically ran the whole Northside of Houston. But that was a story for another time. Right now, I had to deal with Mz. Thickness over there because she wasn't about to let that night go. If she thought I was about to go to jail for that shit, she had better think again.

She gave me that pussy. I didn't ask for it. I didn't take it from her. She gave it to me. As she walked up to the bar, I could see that she was furious. "I need to speak to you," she said through clenched teeth.

Carl, the bartender, who was also a good friend of mine and one of my former soldiers, looked at me. "Everything alright boss?"

"Yea, shit cool. Look, I'm gonna walk this young lady out, but I'll be back soon."

"Aight."

I motioned for Nikola to walk out first and I followed behind her. As I walked out, people were walking in. They all greeted me, and I did the same. Those were people who knew me as the changed man that I was. Nikola was looking at me as someone totally different than the man I was now.

Once outside, I walked her to her car and when we got there, that's when she turned toward me. "I'm gonna need you to explain to me how you thought it was okay to sleep with me that night given the state that I was in."

"You know, I really wish you could remember what happened that night." I said as I ran my hand down my face.

"I had bits and pieces..."

"And? In those bits and pieces, did it seem like I was taking advantage of you?"

"No, but..."

"Look Nikola, I'm sorry that you feel I took advantage of you that night. If I could go back and do it over, I would've driven you home and dropped you on your doorstep. I thought I was doing the right thing by carrying you inside..."

"You carried me inside?"

"Yes, you were kinda passed out snoring, so I picked you up and carried you inside," I said.

"You carried my big ass inside?" she asked as she stared at me in disbelief.

"You aren't that big or heavy."

"Sshhiiiiddd! I know you lie!"

"No really," I said as I walked over to her and scooped her up again. She let out a squeal, but I let her know that I had her and wasn't about to drop her. "See, you aren't that heavy?"

She stared at me with a smile on her face. "You can put me down now," she said as she blushed.

"You sure? I really don't mind holding you like this," I flirted.

"Yes, I'm sure." I placed her back on her feet.

"I'm a good guy Nikola. I didn't do anything to you that night that you didn't want me to." I stepped closer to her. "I can promise you that."

She backed up a little and said, "Well, maybe I misjudged you. It's just that I know I had been drinking and then I woke up naked with you in my bed. That would've freaked any woman out."

"I get it and totally understand. So, now that you aren't trying to kill me anymore, how are you? I mean, how are you feeling about the wedding not going down and shit?" I asked.

"Hey, shit happens right? I'm okay though. It was better to end things before we made a mistake and said I do."

"Well, maybe one day you can tell me about what happened. Right now, I gotta get back inside. You wanna come back in and chill with me?"

"I don't know. I think I've embarrassed myself in there enough for one night. Your bartenders probably think I'm nothing but trouble," she said.

"Well, they are allowed to think what they want. I think you're a beautiful woman and I know that you just got out of a relationship, but I'd like to get to know you better."

"Why?"

"What do you mean, why? I just said that you're beautiful. To be honest, you fascinate me," I said.

"Quit playing," she said as she blushed.

"For real. So, come inside and we can talk and get to know each other. Whaddya say?"

"Okay. Just know that I'm not going to get drunk, so you won't be in my bed in the morning," she said with a laugh.

"Deal," I said as we shook hands.

Whew! At least she wasn't treating me like a rapist anymore. As we walked back to the club, she smiled. I guess she was just as relieved as I was that we didn't have a huge pow wow. Things could've gone totally different if I hadn't lightened the mood by scooping her up.

"Go have a seat and I'll grab you another Shirley Temple." I told her once we were back inside the club.

"Okay." I watched her big butt shake as she went to find a seat.

I walked over to the bar and Carl came over to me. "Everything alright?" he asked with a raised eyebrow.

"Everything is straight. Lemme get a Shirley Temple and a Corona," I said.

"Aye, ain't that the chick that came in last weekend with the wedding dress? The one that didn't get married?"

"Yea, that's her."

"I thought it was. She looks different without the wedding garb, but she still the same size so..." he said as he started laughing. "Man, she is huge!"

"Aye, knock it off aight?"

"C'mon boss man, you can't tell me that you are seriously interested in her. She gon' fuck around and smash yo ass!" Carl said as he cracked up laughing again.

"I said knock it off!" I warned in a more assertive tone. "She's a really nice lady, and she should be treated with respect. I won't have you disrespecting her like that!"

"Sorry boss!"

"You should be." I said as he placed the drinks on the bar. I took them and headed to Nikola's table. I placed her drink in front of her and sat down next to her.

"Are you okay?"

"Yea, I'm straight."

"Thanks for the drink."

"No problem."

"So, how long have you been running this club?" she asked.

"About 15 months," I said.

The two of us sat there and talked for a couple of hours before she decided to leave. I walked her out to her car. "I had a nice time," she said.

"So did I. Maybe you'll let me take you out to dinner one night."

"I'd like that, but I'm not looking for anything serious."

"Understood."

We exchanged numbers and she was on her way.

After communicating through texts and phone calls for the past week, Nikola and I decided to go to dinner. We agreed that I would pick her up and then we'd ride to the restaurant together. I really liked Nikola. She had some issues with her weight and stuff, but I think that had a lot to do with what she told me about her mother. According to Nikola, her mom criticized and ridiculed her every chance she got. I never knew there were parents like that. I just assumed that all parents raised their kids to believe in themselves... to feel good about themselves.

I drove us to Copeland's Seafood Restaurant, and I was every bit the gentleman. I opened the car door for her as well as the door to the restaurant. We were seated immediately and given our menus. As we decided on what we wanted to eat, we gave the server our drink orders.

She ordered a Mardi Gras Punch, so I ordered a Hurricane. I mean, as long as she was ordering a fun drink, I may as well do the same. As we continued to look over the menu, she remarked, "Everything looks so good."

"Everything is good! You haven't been here before?"

"No, but I've always wanted to come here."

"Well, order anything you want," I encouraged.

"Please. I bet you're hoping that I'll order a salad with my big self!"

"Why do you keep putting yourself down like that Nikola? You are a beautiful woman, and you're smart. You should be proud of all you have accomplished in life," I said.

"All that I've accomplished except the title of wifey," she said sadly.

"Hey, you will find someone worthy of a beautiful queen like you one day. The man who you left at the altar didn't deserve you. Trust me, your king is out there. Just be patient."

"Why are you always so nice to me?"

"What do you mean?"

"C'mon Blaze, look at me. You can't really expect me to believe that you're attracted to me. Someone as handsome and as fine as you are, what the hell would you want to do with my big ass?"

"You are really too hard on yourself. Any man, including me, would be lucky to call you his woman. Stop talking so negatively about yourself. If you aren't satisfied with your weight, do something about it. But I think you are beautiful just the way you are," I said.

Her mother had really done a number on her. And the fact that her ex was cheating on her with another dude didn't help her ego either. If she allowed me to, I'd help her to see just how lucky any man would be to have her in their life. She just needed some encouragement to get past all the shit she had endured in the past.

"Are you all ready to order?" the server asked as she placed our drinks before us.

"I'll have the Pasta Shrimp Copeland with a side order of the gumbo," Nikola said.

"Would you like the cup or the bowl of gumbo?"

"The cup please."

"And for you sir?"

"I'll have the seafood platter with a cup of gumbo please," I said.

"Okay. I'll put those orders right in," she said and walked away.

"Nikola, if we gon' keep hanging out like this, I'm gonna need you to stop doubting yourself. I wish you could see what I see when I look at you."

"And what is that... Shamu the whale, a great white shark?"

"Wow! Is that really what you see when you look at yourself in the mirror?"

"Sometimes."

"Well damn! What kind of mirror you got... one of those fun house mirrors?" I asked as we busted out laughing.

"Boy, stop!"

"I'm serious. We gonna have to get you a new mirror if that's the image reflecting when you look into it. What I see from sitting here is a beautiful, voluptuous, and vivacious woman. And you wanna know something else?"

"What?"

I leaned in closer to her and whispered. "You rocked my damn world that other night."

She leaned back in her seat and stared at me. "Ha! HA!" she said.

"What's funny?"

"You are."

"I wasn't trying to be. I'm dead ass serious."

"Whatever."

"You don't believe me?" I asked.

"Nope."

"Lemme prove it to you."

"What? What do you mean by that?"

"Give me another chance to prove it to you," I offered.

"Oh, uh uh, you are some slick..." I stood up from the table and made my way to her side of the booth. "Where are you going?"

"Move over," I said.

"Go sit down Blaze!"

"Move over," I repeated. She blushed as she looked around the restaurant. A few heads had turned in our direction, so she scooted over in her seat.

I wasn't trying to scare her or anything, but instead, I wanted to boost her ego and self- esteem. I put my arm around her shoulder. "Um, what are you doing?"

"Ssshhh!" I shushed with my finger to my lips. I took that same finger and placed it under her chin before pressing my lips to hers. I could feel her nervousness as her body trembled next to me.

"Nikola?" someone asked.

She jumped and pressed her hand to her lips as she stared into my eyes. "I didn't say anything," I said as we turned in the direction of the voice.

There were two dudes standing near our table eyeing us both down like we were pieces of meat, well me anyway. Nikola blew out an exasperated breath and rolled her eyes as she looked at the dudes.

"Well, hello," one of the dudes' greeted.

"I see you've recovered well," one of the dudes' said.

"Sure did!" Nikola responded with a smirk.

"Go on girl. Shit, I ain't mad atcha, in my 2Pac voice!"

I wondered who the hell these dudes were. Like, didn't they see us enjoying each other's company? I turned my attention to Nikola. "Um, you wanna introduce me to your friends?" I asked.

"Oh, they aren't my friends. That's the dude I was supposed to marry," she said pointing to the dude on the left. "That's the dude he was screwing behind my back!" She pointed to the other dude who was looking around, I guess trying to see if anyone was watching what was transpiring.

"Ooohh," I said as I nodded my head.

Damn! This night had just gotten hella interesting. I was confused though. I'm sitting here looking at the dude she was supposed to marry and wondering why she didn't know he had sugar in his tank. The nigga even stood like he was fruity. How didn't she know?

Oh well... his lost!

Chapter eight

Charles

The past couple of weeks had been horrible. I didn't lose my job, thank God. But I didn't get the promotion that I wanted either. After sulking for the past two weeks about the failed promotion, Jerry suggested we go out. He said we didn't have to act like we were together, but rather just two friends going to dinner. The only reason I agreed was because I was bored. So, we decided to meet at Copeland's Seafood. I hadn't been there in ages and I thought it would be just the thing I needed to get me out of this funk that I was in.

We walked in and were seated in a quiet corner booth. The two of us had ordered and were enjoying our meal when I noticed Nikola walk in with some dude. Imagine the surprised look on my face when I saw her out with another man so soon after the break up. I just assumed she'd be at home crying because I knew that I had hurt her. I really had put her through some shit, and I knew how much she was in love with me.

The way she was eyeing the dude didn't look like she gave two shits about me. When Jerry caught me glancing in that direction, of course he was curious as to what I was looking at. When his eyes followed mine and he saw who I was looking at, I could sense that we were going to argue. The affection that I used to show Nikola in public was something that Jerry dreamed about. But I wasn't ready for that kind of shit with him.

What the hell was going on?

"Well, what is going on over there? Looks like Nikola done moved on," Jerry said. "Mmmm! And he is a cutie pie!"

"Shut up Jerry!"

"Why you telling me to shut up? I'm just saying that the dude looks good. Oh my gawd! And you thought that girl was sitting at home whining and crying over you. Clearly that ain't what she's been doing at all!" he teased with a smile.

"Jerry..."

"Jerry what? What... you mad cuz she done moved on? Shit, ain't that what you told her you were doing?"

"No, that's what you told her I was doing. You made that decision for me," I said.

"Oh yea! Well, that's because I was tired of being locked up in that little closet. I'on know whatchu mad at. You wasn't even attracted to her big ass anyway!"

"You don't know shit about her! She's a good woman."

"Big women like her are always good. That's because they insecure as fuck! Shit, she knew ain't nobody else wanted that big ol' ass!" Jerry said. "Well, at least that's what I thought. Obviously, somebody else does want her. You go head on Nikola!"

"Shut up Jerry!"

"Boy, I swear, if you tell me shut up one more fucking time..."

"Well, stop talking shit then!" I said. He was really annoying the hell out of me right now. I wasn't expecting Nikola to be here, and I certainly didn't expect to see her with no dude.

"Let's go say hello," Jerry suggested, being messy.

"Nah, I'm good."

As I watched the dude stand up and slide into the booth Nikola was sitting in, my mouth dropped when they started kissing like teenagers. "Well damn! Shit, she sho' ain't worried about yo ass at all!" Jerry teased. "He got his tongue all up and through. Get it boy. Umph, umph, umph! I am so jealous right now."

"C'mon!" I said.

"Where we going?"

"We're leaving!" I said.

"I ain't finished eating," he said being stubborn.

I stood up and of course, he followed. We began walking toward the door. On the way to the door, we had to pass by Nikola's table. I couldn't just walk by and say nothing if I wanted to because my feet wouldn't let me.

We stood near the table waiting for them to notice us and when they didn't, I had to say something. "Nikola?"

The two of them finally came up for air. She looked at me and rolled her eyes. She didn't even look the least bit embarrassed that I had seen her.

"Well, hello," I greeted with a tight smile.

"I see you've recovered well," Jerry said. It took everything in me not to snatch his ass. Why the hell was he making shit more awkward than what it already was?

"Sure did!" Nikola responded as she smiled with a smirk.

"Go on girl. Shit, I ain't mad atcha, in my 2Pac voice!" Jerry said.

"Um, you wanna introduce me to your friends?" asked the dude who just had his tongue down her throat.

"Oh, they aren't my friends. That's the dude I was supposed to marry," she said as she pointed her finger in my direction. "Oh, and that's the dude he was screwing behind my back!" She pointed in Jerry's direction.

"Ooohh," the dude said.

"Actually, I'm Charles and this is Jerry," I said.

"Blaze," the dude said.

"Blaze? Like a sparkling fire?" Jerry asked as he smiled stupidly.

"Don't you two have somewhere to be? I mean, we'd like to be alone," Nikola said.

Damn. I knew she was still bitter, but I never thought she would act this way. She had always been so sweet to me. This was something new that I didn't really like, but what the hell could I do or say? I had fucked up her life. I was surprised she was even speaking to me.

The server came to her table, so we backed up.

"It was nice seeing you, Nikola. Nice meeting you Blaze." I said as I stuck my hand out to shake his.

He looked at my hand and said, "Yea, aight."

Jerry said, "Well, looks like things worked out for the best for you Nikola. Glad to see you happy again."

"Happy period!" Nikola said.

"Excuse me," Jerry said.

"I'm finally happy. I thought I was happy with Charles, but I really wasn't. Blaze makes me super happy," she said as she kissed the dude right in front of me.

"Well, take care." I said as me and Jerry headed for the door.

As soon as we got outside, he started going in. "Well damn, I'd say that Nikola has bounced back really well!"

"Yea," I said as I headed to my car.

"So, you want me to come over or you coming to my place?"

"Actually Jerry, I'm kind of tired. I'll talk to you tomorrow, okay?" I said, not bothering to wait for a response.

I slid in my car and headed out of the parking lot. I'd be lying if I said seeing Nikola with that dude didn't have me feeling some kind of way. I knew I had no right to feel anything, but I did. She needed to move on because I did, so why wasn't I happy about that?

Jerry really made shit awkward as hell. It was almost like he wanted to piss me off or something. He had better watch it because he was replaceable.

Chapter nine

Nikola

The last two people I expected to see at this restaurant were Charles and Jerry. After what they did, I had high hopes that I'd never see them again. However, God had other plans. Let me start off with the kiss that Blaze gave me. That kiss had started a fire from the top of my head to the bottom of my damn feet. When he started flirting with me, I had no idea it would lead to some steamy interaction between the two of us. He and I had flirted by phone and through texts for the past week, but I never thought anything of it.

After the botched wedding, I wasn't feeling in the best of spirits. I usually had so much confidence and a helluva lot of self-esteem. But once another man had left me at the altar, so to speak, I just lost everything that I ever believed myself to be. I used to look at myself in the mirror and what I'd see was a woman who could have any man she wanted to regardless of what size I was.

I had tried so many times to lose the weight, but I couldn't do it. I had failed so many diets and exercise regimens that I didn't have the strength to go through another one. I had been through so many disappointments in my life that I was afraid to go through life anymore. I wasn't sure how many more I could go through. My entire life had been filled with people who had let me down. I was afraid to trust people anymore.

When Blaze, whose real name I found out was Lincoln Watson, first invited me out to dinner, I had declined. The last thing I needed was another man in my life who had the opportunity to let me down. I wasn't going to believe or trust in one more man that could break my heart. Blaze and I continued to chat and text and I found myself liking him. The thug that I thought he was wasn't the man he showed me he was. I started thinking that I might have misjudged him.

After having him ask me two more times, I finally agreed. When I told Trinity that Blaze had asked me out, she encouraged me to go.

"You don't think it's too soon?" I asked.

"Too soon for what?" she asked which I found confusing.

"For me to go on a date! I mean, I just ended things with Charles two weeks ago."

"Girl bye! Was it too soon for him to jump back in bed with Jerry after y'all ended things?" She had a point.

Charles was probably living his best life with Jerry's ass while I was out there doubting whether I should go out on one date. One date with a man who had made me smile and laugh more in one week than I had in months.

"I guess you're right," I said.

"You know that I'm right. Charles was an ass who didn't deserve to be loved by you. You have a lot to offer any man in a relationship. Where was all that confidence you possessed not that long ago?"

"I don't have anything to be confident about."

"You have every reason to be confident in yourself. Nikki you are a beautiful woman. Don't let your size have you thinking you're not worthy to be loved. You are talented and sexy and very vivacious. Any man would be lucky to have you as his woman, and don't you ever forget that shit!"

This is what I loved about Trinity. She always had a way to make me feel special. That's why she was my best friend. "So, you really think I should go out with him?"

"Hell yes! If anything, you will get a good free meal out of it," she chuckled.

"Okay, but if things don't work out..."

"Just don't get drunk."

"I won't," I said as we shared a laugh together.

We ended the call and I called Blaze back and accepted the date. I was shocked as hell when he came and sat next to me and started kissing me right there in the restaurant in front of anyone who was watching. I was in for an even bigger shock when Charles and Jerry made their presence known. Like what the fuck would make them think it was okay to stop at my table? I hadn't seen Jerry since the wedding, and I hadn't seen Charles since he popped up at my house.

Why would they think it was cool to be here? They should've known that I didn't have anything to say to them and that I wouldn't want to see them. After I read their asses, I stuck my tongue back in Blaze's mouth which surprised even me. They finally walked away from the table and I pulled back from Blaze.

"I'm so sorry..."

"You have no reason to apologize."

"Yes, I do. I don't want you to feel like I'm using you to get back at Charles."

"Was that what you were doing... trying to make your ex jealous?"

"Hell no!" I shrieked. "I guess I just wanted him to think that I had moved on. I wanted him to see that he didn't break me even though we didn't get married."

"I totally understand. I have no problem with kissing you, Nikola. Feel free to do that whenever you feel like it," he smiled.

"Thanks, but I think you better move back over to your side before our food gets cold."

"You're right."

He slid out of the booth and the two of us conversed while we ate.

"Would it bother you if I called you Lincoln?"

"Not at all. I mean, it is my given name. You don't like Blaze?" he asked with a smile.

"I'm not gonna say all that. I just like the way Lincoln rolls of my tongue," I smiled back.

"Shit, I like the way it rolls off your tongue too."

"You're so silly."

"I like that I can be silly with you. Most people don't get to see this side of me."

"Why not? Because you're hard?" I asked.

"Not really because I'm hard, but because when people see me acting a certain way, they won't take me seriously. I just choose to keep things as professional and business like as possible."

"I get that. Have you ever been married?"

"Yea, it didn't work out."

"Sorry to hear that," I said. That was the first time I had ever inquired about his marital status. I never thought to ask about that because he wasn't wearing a ring. I honestly don't know what made me ask that question.

"It's cool. There aren't any hard feelings between us... shit just didn't work out."

"Do y'all have kids together?"

"I have a son."

"Wow! How old is he?"

"He's seven," he admitted.

"Does he live with your ex?"

"Yes, they live in Houston."

"Oh, right. You did say that's where you were from," I remembered.

"Yea."

"Do you get to see him often?"

"Not as often as I would like, but I see him."

"What's his name?" I asked.

"Lincoln Desean Watson Jr., but we just call him L.J. for short."

"Cool."

We continued to chat until our food was gone. Once he paid the tab, we left. He opened the door for me, and I slid into the comfortable seat. He got behind the wheel and we headed back to my place.

"I had a great time," I said with a smile.

"So did I. I'd like to take you out again if you're up for it."

"Really?"

"Yes really."

"Well, just say when," I smiled happily.

I needed to remind myself that just because we were going out didn't mean anything was starting between us. We were just two friends who enjoyed each other's company. Nothing more and nothing less.

"Well, I have to go out of town tomorrow, but maybe we can get together next weekend."

"Yea, sure. I'd like that."

He pulled into the parking lot of my complex and parked near my building. He got out and walked me to the door. "I'll hit you up when I get back," he said.

"Okay, sounds good."

"I really had a great time tonight."

"I did too. I'm glad I agreed to the date," I said.

"I'm glad too."

He pulled me close to him and planted his lips on mine. I realized that I had wanted him to kiss me. If he hadn't done it, I would've been really disappointed. I opened my mouth to receive his soft tongue. If felt amazing to be kissing this man. As his hands stroked my back, his tongue drove deeper inside my mouth.

When I felt my panties sticking to me, I knew they were getting moist, so I slightly pushed him away.

"Are you okay?" he asked.

"Mmm hmm," I responded, scared of what I'd say if I opened my mouth.

"Aight. I'll hit you up when I get back in town."

"Okay."

He pecked me again on the lips before heading back to his truck. I went inside and leaned against the door. That man had literally caused me to cream in my panties from just a kiss. *No man had ever done that to me before. Good Lord,* I thought.

I went to my bedroom to get ready for bed. My phone began to ring as soon as I got in bed. I assumed it was Lincoln so of course I answered.

"Hey," I said trying to sound sexy.

"I'm glad you answered the phone." The smile I just had on my face dropped instantly. I pulled the phone from my ear and looked at the screen.

"What the hell do you want Charles? I mean, didn't you say what you needed to say when I saw you earlier?"

"Nikki..."

"DON'T CALL ME THAT! MY NAME IS NIKOLA! NIKOLA! N-I-K-O-L-A! YOU GOT IT?!" I yelled. He didn't have the right to call me Nikki anymore.

He lost that right when he started fucking Jerry.

"I'm sorry. I'm sorry. I'm just used to calling you Nikki."

"You lost that right to call me Nikki! You are to refer to me as Nikola! Why the hell are you calling me anyway?"

"I just needed to apologize to you again. I'm so sorry things didn't work out between us, but if you could just give me another chan..."

"Nigga, I know you ain't about to ask me to give you another damn chance! After you been fucking a man! I know you ain't fixing your mouth to say those words to me!"

I had no idea what his intentions were when he called me, but I wasn't about to listen to that shit. I never want to be with Charles again in my life. What part of that didn't he get?

"In case you haven't noticed, I've moved on. If you thought that was just a show for you, you're wrong. I didn't even know that you were there. I already got a man and he is a real MAN!"

"What's that supposed to mean?"

"It means he doesn't bend over during sex, only me."

"Nikola please, I just want to prove to you that I can be the man you want me to be."

"The fact that you said that means that you don't even know who you are," I said. "What we had is over. I don't want you."

"I still love you though," he said.

"You never loved me boy! You can't love a woman when you're fucking a man!"

"I can be the man you thought I was. Just forget what Jerry said..."

"Dude what the fuck?! How the hell can I ever forget what Jerry said? Hell, the whole town was present when you came out of the closet!"

"I didn't come out of the closet though! Jerry said some bullshit, and everybody just ran with it. I hadn't said anything at all about coming out of any closet. Please, take me back!"

"Okay, this isn't going anywhere. Hear me and hear me good. WE ARE OVER!!" I said. I didn't want to shout or anything like that because I had a good evening, matter of fact a great evening with Lincoln. I wasn't trying to mar it with this shit that Charles was speaking of. "Look, I'm not about to get upset after the evening I just had. I'm going to need you to forget all these thoughts of us getting back together out of your head. We are done. I would never be with a man who was not only unfaithful to me, but sleeping with a man. You know I had to get tested to make sure you hadn't given me any kind of disease?"

"Of course, I wouldn't have given you any diseases! I'm not stupid Nikola!"

"Whatever Charles! I just want you to stay out of my life. I have a man and he's 100% into me. So, you do you and I'll do me, and we won't ever have this conversation again. Take care Charles. Tell Jerry I said thanks for not letting me make the biggest mistake of my life."

"Nikola please, we can work this out. I know you still love me," he pleaded.

My phone beeped signaling another call was coming through. I looked at the caller ID and smiled when I saw Lincoln's name and handsome face pop up.

I busted out laughing. "Boy bye! Any love I had for you went out the window as soon as I found out you were fucking Jerry, or he was fucking you... however that shit went! Anyway, my man is on the other line, so don't call my phone no mo'! Got it!" I ended the call because I couldn't put up with him for one more minute.

"Hey," I said after I clicked the phone over.

"Hey yourself. How are you?"

"I'm okay. You make it home alright?"

"Nah, I'm actually about to walk in the club. I had to come by and check on things before I head home."

"Oh okay. Well, don't let me keep you," I said.

"You're not. I just wanted to hear your voice before you go to sleep."

"Aw, that's sweet."

"I can have my moments," he said. I could hear him smiling in his voice, which only made me blush.

What was I doing? Why was I flirting so heavily with this man when I knew that I wasn't ready for another relationship so soon? He was just easy to talk to and very likable.

"Did you have a good time tonight?" I asked.

"You know I did. I enjoy spending time with you," he said.

"Do you really?"

"Yea, why wouldn't I?"

"No reason."

"Are you in bed?"

"Yep."

"What are your plans for tomorrow?"

"I was just gonna relax, maybe clean house," I said.

"Oh, aight. Maybe we can chill tomorrow," he suggested.

"Maybe. Hit me up when you get a chance," I said.

"I will."

"Have a good night Lincoln and be safe."

"Aight mami."

I couldn't stop smiling even after we ended the call. That was the first time he called me mami and I liked it. I got off the phone that night feeling like a million bucks. I got out of bed and went to stand in front of the mirror in my bathroom. As I stared at my reflection, I smiled because I was starting to see what Lincoln and Trinity saw in me. I was starting to see just how beautiful I was.

Yea, I was a little plump, but my face was beautiful. Yes, I may have a little extra fat around my midsection, but my butt was round and on point. Sure, my arms were a little bigger than I needed them to be, but it matched the rest of my body. My breasts were big and bold and with the right bra could leave any man's mouth open. Yea, I was a big, voluptuous and sexy female.

"I am big, bold, and beautiful. I am big, bold, and beautiful. I AM BIG, BOLD, AND BEAUTIFUL!" Those were the words Trinity taught me about myself. She said I didn't have to be a size two or 12 to be beautiful. Lincoln said I was beautiful no matter what size I was. Thank God I was starting to believe that again. I needed to believe that.

I turned the bathroom light off and hopped back in the king sized bed. I placed my phone on the charger and turned the bedside lamp off. I closed my eyes and wasn't surprised when sleep came easy. I had been up since five this morning working on designs for websites for my clients and I was exhausted. I worked for a web design company and not to toot my own horn, but I was one of their top three web designers at the firm. I made good money doing web designs.

I had a great place to live, a nice car, and a fantastic job. The only thing I was missing was a good man in my life. I wasn't sure where this thing between Lincoln and I, but I wasn't ready for anything serious. I didn't know if I'd ever be able to allow another man close to my heart again. Maybe Lincoln and I could be friends... hell, maybe even friends with benefits. That way no one's heart was involved and neither of us would be expecting anything.

I just didn't wanna think of us in that way just yet. Thinking of Lincoln before I went to sleep had me dreaming about him again. Those dreams of him and I having sex always seemed to invade my nightly thoughts. I didn't know what I was going to do about those thoughts.

I definitely wouldn't mind feeling him inside me again...

Chapter ten

Blaze
Two months later...

Me and Nikola were still kicking it. We hadn't had sex
since that first night, but it was cool. She had been
dumped at the altar by a dude who was confused about
his sexuality. She mentioned that he had called her a
couple of times begging to get back with her. I found
that odd that a man who had another man as his lover
would still want to be with a woman. That dude needed
counseling if you asked me. I mean, why beg a woman
you intended to marry to get back with you if you were
sleeping with some other nigga? That shit was all the
way nasty to me. No wonder Nikki didn't want to fuck
no other niggas right now. I was more than sure she was
confused as fuck.

With that being said, I had no reason to expect the
dude to show up at my club tonight. I mean, he was
welcomed here. I had nothing against him. However, I
suspected he wasn't here for that jazz music that was
coming from the band on stage. As he walked over to my
table, I instantly got in defense mode. I mean, why was

he here? He didn't know me and from what I knew of him, I didn't really like him.

"Hey," he greeted as he stood near my table.

"S'up?" I greeted with a head nod as I downed my glass of scotch.

"I was wondering if we could have a conversation."

"About what?"

"Nikola, of course."

"Why do we need to have a conversation about Nikola?" I asked as I stared him up and down.

"May I sit down?"

"Do what you need to do man," I said. He sat down and looked around nervously, almost like he was looking for someone. "Your boyfriend joining you?"

"He's not my boyfriend," he said through clenched teeth.

"Look man, whatever is going on between y'all ain't my business. Frankly, I don't even know why you're here."

"I need you to back off Nikola."

"Whatchu mean back off?"

"I mean, I need you to leave her alone," he rephrased.

"Why would I do that?" I asked.

"Because she won't give me another shot as long as you're in the picture."

I cracked up laughing so hard that I almost fell out of my chair. This nigga was really funny. He thought that I was going to back away from Nikola because he asked me... so he could have another chance to shoot his shot. This nigga was really buggin' and he was confused.

"Dude really?"

"Yes really! As long as she's dating you, she'll never give me a chance."

"Dude, even if I backed off, Nikki has made it very clear that she doesn't want shit to do with you," I informed him. This dude had to be delusional or something.

"She will, if she's feeling lonely enough," he said.

Wow! I ain't never had no nigga come at me this way. He actually wanted me to break things off with Nikola, so she would be lonely enough to take him back. That's some bullshit!

"Nigga, you tried it!" I said as I cracked up again. All of a sudden, the other dude Jerry walked over to the table.

Charles instantly became uneasy.

"Hey, what's going on here?" Jerry asked.

"Nothing. Just came by to check out Blaze's club," Charles lied. "I told you that I heard his club was jumping and you know how much I like jazz."

"Mmm hmm," Jerry said with a face that showed he probably didn't believe what Charles was saying. "So, this is really your spot Blaze?"

"Yea."

"The band is fresh," Jerry said as he started doing a two-step. "Yea, this band is dope! Charles come dance with me!"

"Yea Charles, go dance with your boyfriend," I said as I got up and walked away.

I headed to the storage room to call Nikola because I knew this was going to blow her mind.

"Hey Lincoln, what's going on? Are you at the club?" she asked when she answered.

"Yea and you are never going to guess who's over here," I said with a laugh.

"Who? You know me and Trinity are on our way over there, right?"

"Yea, I just wanted to give you a heads up before you got here."

"Oh boy! Who's over there?" she asked.

"Charles and Jerry," I said.

"What? Charles and Jerry?" she asked in disbelief. "You're kidding right?"

"No, I'm not."

"Well, we're about to pull in the parking lot right now," she said.

"Okay, I'll come out to meet y'all."

I walked out of the storage room to find Jerry still cutting up the dance floor while Charles sat at the table nursing a drink. Jerry was twerking and showing out like crazy. I was stunned. I walked out the building as Trinity and Blaze were walking toward the door. I hugged them both and kissed Nikki.

"That dude Jerry is really cuttin' up!" I said.

"What?" Nikki asked as she cracked a smile.

"Just wait until y'all get inside."

So, we walked back inside, and Jerry was still on the dance floor twirling and shit. When Charles spotted Nikki, he rushed over to us. "Hey Nikola, Trinity... I didn't know y'all were coming here," Charles said.

"Why would you know?" Trinity asked. "We don't answer to you."

"Look Trinity, I know you don't care about me..."

"Don't, didn't, never will..." Trinity responded.

"Wow! Okay, I get it. So, Nikola can we talk?"

"No! I came over here to have a good time with my BFF and my man!" Nikola said.

"Please..."

"Well, hey there y'all!" Jerry said as he draped an arm around Charles' shoulder. Charles brushed his hand off which caused Jerry to catch an attitude. "What the fuck?"

"I already told you not to do that shit in public!" Charles said.

"We're a couple now, so it shouldn't even matter who sees us now!" Jerry said.

"We are not a couple. I don't know how many times I have to tell you that!"

"Oh, so we're not a couple, but we sleep in the same bed," Jerry said.

As Nikola, Trinity and I watched their exchange, it took everything I had not to throw up. The thought of two men getting it on wasn't something I was interested in hearing. So, I excused myself with some excuse about checking on my customers. I didn't know what the hell was going on, but I knew Nikola wanted nothing to do with Charles or Jerry. I made sure to watch out for her because if any of those little niggas got flip with their lip, I was going to throw them out on their ass.

I continued to watch the exchange between Charles and Jerry get a little heated. I did a head nod to the bouncer for him to escort them out. That was the kind of shit I didn't need in my club. My club catered to a more mature crowd because I didn't like bullshit and drama from the younger generation. Even though I was only 30-years old, I had been through a lot in my life. Because of everything I had been through, some people thought that I was an old soul in a young body. I took that as a compliment.

So, Brutus approached the two of them, said some words and escorted them out. If I didn't know any better, I would've sworn that Jerry was coming on to Brutus. But he was definitely barking up the wrong tree if he thought that my security guard was going to bite his little apple.

Nikki and Trinity took their seats and a short time later, I joined them. Trinity's man, Jason joined us about an hour later and the four of us took to the dance floor. Once we got rid of Charles and Jerry, we had a great time.

Hours later, I drove Nikola home. I walked her to the door, and she invited me in. I was a bit surprised because she hadn't invited me in since she had thrown me out three months ago. I sat on the sofa while she disappeared into the bedroom. She returned with her hair flowing over her shoulder and she had traded in her heels for a pair of house slippers. She sat down next to me and offered me something to drink. I declined because I wasn't thirsty.

"You seem nervous?" I remarked.

"I guess I am a little nervous."

"Why are you nervous?"

"I don't know. I guess because I invited you in."

"That's not a reason to be nervous," I said.

"I wanna have sex!" she blurted.

Nah, I just knew I hadn't heard her right. Did she just say she wanted to have sex?

"Um, with me?"

"Do you see anyone else around?" she asked. "I mean, if you don't want to..."

I kissed the rest of her sentence away. Of course, I wanted to. To be honest, I didn't know how I was this attracted to Nikola. I had never been with a woman her size before, but I looked past her size when I was with her. Not that her size bothered me or anything. I was aware of her fluff and rolls from the beginning. But Nikola was a beautiful woman, so those rolls didn't matter when we were together.

While she was the thickest I had ever been with, she was also the softest. Her skin was as soft as a newborn's ass and she always smelled so good. Her insides were moist and had made gushy noises when I plowed in and out of her. Damn! That day she had thrown me out, I wished she hadn't because at the time I was looking forward to blessing her with another serving of that good wood.

Here I was and she was giving me another chance. I pulled back from kissing her to ask a couple of questions.

"Are you sure?" I asked.

"Yes, I'm sure... unless you don't want to."

"No, I want to. I just want to make sure you ain't gonna kick me out in the morning."

"Oh, so you got jokes," she said with a laugh.

"Uh, not really."

"Well, I promise not to throw you out in the morning. As a matter of fact, if your performance is good, I may just cook you breakfast."

"Shit, you ain't said but a word," I said.

She stood up and reached for my hand, leading me to her bedroom. Once in the bedroom, I slowly undressed her. As she stood before me in her bra and panties, I could see that she was a little shy. I tilted her chin upward and said, "You don't have to look away from me. I want you."

I could see the relief in her face as I brought my lips to hers. She reached for my shirt and lifted it over my head. I liked that she was taking the initiative to do that. She stared at my abs and ran her finger along the cut on my stomach. "What happened?"

"We can talk about that later," I said as I slowly pushed her on the bed. I removed her panties and tossed them to the floor.

I also removed her bra, allowing her big boobs to fall out. Her boobs were big, but they still had a bit of bounce to them. Nikola was only 25, so I didn't expect her boobs to fall in her lap. I kissed her lips then traveled my lips to her breasts. I wrapped my lips around one of them and sucked it as my tongue teased her swollen nipple. I pinched the nipple on her other boob as she moaned deeply.

I moved downward and kissed her fluffy belly. Before I put my mouth on her pussy, she stopped me. "Wait!" she cried, panting breathlessly. "Wh-wh-what are you doing?"

"You'll see," I said as I smiled and disappeared between her legs.

Damn her pussy was a big ol' fat cat. I had never been face to puss with a cat of this magnitude, but I was going to pretend it was a big slice of meatloaf... my favorite food. I slid my tongue between her crevices and immediately felt her cream on my tongue. I continued to slide my tongue in and out of her hole and up and down her lips, sucking on her fat nub from time to time. She moaned loudly as her body shook over and over again. This was something I hadn't done to Nikki the first time. I knew damn well she wasn't gon' throw me out in the morning.

Hell, she probably wouldn't even want me to leave. When I felt her legs lock on my face, I suddenly felt as if I was smothering. I softly slapped the side of her leg for her to open it. She did and I stood up, gasping for air. Damn! I saw my life flash before my eyes in the five seconds she had me trapped.

"Are you okay?" she asked, a worried expression on her face.

I didn't want to ruin the mood by worrying her, so I played it off. "Yea, I'm good."

"I'm so sorry," she said. "I just never had anyone do that to me before."

Shit, I believed her. If she had, I was sure I would've read about them being deceased.

I couldn't help but smile as I removed my pants and boxers. I reached in my back pocket and pulled out a Magnum condom. I stroked my dick as she watched it grow.

"I'd offer to return the favor, but I don't have any experience in that department," she admitted shyly.

"It's cool."

This was really different. Usually women knew exactly what to do with my dick. I was sure that Nikki was just a little inexperienced, which was fine with me. I mean, I'd rather have a chick who ain't never sucked a dick before as opposed to a chick who was a pro at sucking the dick. I removed the condom from the wrapper and rolled it on my erect shaft.

Then I climbed on top of her and teased the opening of her pussy with the head of my dick. "Oh my God!" she crooned.

When I finally stuffed her fat cat with my beef stick, she was soaking wet. There went the gushy noises I remembered hearing the first time. Her pussy felt amazing. It was tight and wet and damn! I found myself ready to bust a nut within minutes, but I wasn't about to go out like no punk! No pun to the other niggas... Charles and Jerry!

Chapter eleven

Jerry

I asked Charles if he wanted to go out tonight, but he said no. I wasn't surprised though because he had been running from me since the night we ran into Nikola tonguing down Mr. Fine Ass in Copeland's. Yea, that's right. I said he was fine because he was. I could see why Nikola moved on so fast. Shit, I wished he was gay or bisexual, I would've moved on from Charles too.

The fresh haircut alone made my mouth water then he was tall too. He was about 6'4, weighed approximately 225 pounds and baby, he was slim, trim and well put together. His chestnut brown eyes twinkled when he laughed. And the trim of his moustache and goatee framed his face to perfection. He looked like a honey colored God.

I had discreetly placed a tracker on Charles' car... don't judge me. I had worked too hard to get that dude in my clutches for him to not act right. So, when I saw his car parked at the blues and jazz club, I got dressed and headed over there. I had spoken to him earlier and he said he wasn't going anywhere because he was tired.

If he was that tired, why the hell was he at the club? When I walked in and saw him sitting there with Mr. Fine Ass himself, my mouth almost hit the floor.

What the hell was he doing here and with him? I thought that was Nikola's new man. Humph, or was that just a rouse to throw me off?

As I sauntered over there looking all cute, I became a little enraged. However, I had way too much class to show out in public. The last thing I wanted to do was give people a reason to start talking shit about me and Charles. So, I plastered a huge smile on my face and went over to say hello. Dude looked uncomfortable as fuck, especially when I started dancing. Charles also looked uncomfortable, probably because I had caught him in a lie.

I wanted to say something to him about his ass being here... I mean, since he was so tired and all. The party really got interesting when Nikola and her bestie walked in. Charles jumped out of his seat and rushed over there.

"Like what the fuck?" I said as I watched him acting the fool.

I was really tired of him disrespecting me. We were supposed to be in a monogamous relationship. Sure, he still had problems admitting he was gay to other people. But I know that he knew he was gay. What was the problem coming out of the closet? I mean, wouldn't it be better to be yourself than to live a lie?

I walked over there and of course, since Charles was my man, I draped my arm around his shoulders.

"Well, hey there y'all!" What do you think he did? That nigga shook my arm off him. What the hell kind of shit was that? I was tired of not saying shit, so of course, I popped off. "What the fuck?"

"I already told you not to do that shit in public!" he said with an attitude.

"We're a couple now, so it shouldn't even matter who sees us now!" I retorted back.

"We are not a couple. I don't know how many times I have to tell you that!"

I didn't know if he was saying that because he was still ashamed of who he really was, but I didn't give a shit. He and I slept in the same bed four out of seven days of the week. Whether he wanted to admit it or not, we were a fucking couple! I was sick and tired of him downplaying our relationship.

"Oh, so we're not a couple, but we sleep in the same bed," I remarked. "You slap it, flip it and rub it down several nights a week, but we ain't a couple. Humph, okay!"

That must have been too much info for Mr. Fine Ass because he walked away.

"T.M.I." Nikola said as she and Trinity laughed.

"I'm just saying! He needs to stop lying for whatever reason!" I said in frustration.

"You can really be honest about your relationship with Jerry, Charles. We aren't together anymore, nor are we ever getting back together. With that being said, you have no reason to deny your feelings for your lover," Nikola said.

"There! Everybody knows we're together, so what's the problem?"

"I'm not going to make a scene in here, but we are not together," Charles said.

"We're together," I whispered in a joking manner, but I was as serious as a heart attack.

"Well, we're going to let the two of you enjoy your evening," Nikola said.

"Nikola, can we please have a conversation in private?" Charles asked.

"No Charles! I don't want to have a conversation with you in private or in public! All I want is for you to leave me alone. I told you already that we are never getting back together! So please, just leave it alone and move on!" Nikola said.

What the fuck was Nikola talking about? And why the hell did Charles need to speak with her in private? What the fuck was going on?

Before Nikola could walk off, I stopped her. "Nikola, excuse me girl."

She and Trinity turned to face me. "What Jerry?"

"What do you mean by the two of you aren't getting back together? Everybody knows y'all aren't getting back together after y'all wedding flopped!" I said.

"Something you had everything to do with," Trinity said.

"Guilty as charged, boo! I would think that the two of you would be happy knowing the truth," I said.

"Oh, I'm very happy that you came forward with the truth. I even told Charles to thank you for that. You saw my man right? Trust me, I'm very happy and com-plete-ly satisfied!" Nikola said as she and Trinity gave each other a high five.

"Right, but has Charles asked you to get back together? That's what I wanna know," I said.

"Jerry why are you inquiring shit like that. That's your problem. You're always assuming shit!" Charles said.

"Oh, no you won't be making me feel as if this shit is in my head! I just heard Nikola say that you need to stop asking her to get back together. If you are asking her that behind my back, what the hell are we doing? I thought we were in a relationship! I mean, Nikola is out of your life and everyone knows that we are fucking! So,

I'm kinda lost here," I said. "Shit, I feel like one of Little Bo Peep's sheep right about now! Can somebody please find me and point me in the right damn direction? I'm looking for the truth!"

As that moment, the security guard walked over to us to escort us out. "Why the fuck we gotta leave? Ain't this a public place for anybody to attend?"

"It is, but y'all are causing drama and we don't do that here. So, if you two will leave on your own, I'd appreciate it. Because I really don't wanna have to throw y'all out," he said.

"Have a good night guys," Nikola said as her and Trinity walked away.

I crossed my arms over my chest in typical angry queen fashion and marched out the door. Charles followed behind me and he was pissed. But if he thought he was mad, bayyybbbeee! He ain't seen mad yet!

"You bastard!" I said as I turned on him.

He just rolled his eyes and said, "I don't have time for this shit! That's your fucking problem now... you're always trying to make a scene and shit! How did you even know I was here?"

"Don't worry about how I knew you were here! I found you didn't I?" I asked. "Why the hell would you try and get back with One Ton Wanda when we're supposed to be in a relationship?"

"Don't call her that! And we aren't in a re-la-tion-SHIP!! You want a relationship with me, but I have a huge problem with that!"

"What's the problem now? One Ton Wanda is out of the way, so now what's the issue?"

"I'M NOT GAY!! You keep trying to turn me into someone I'm not and will never be!"

"You are gay, stop fighting it!"

"I'm not fighting shit! Okay, we had sex... I guess I was curious..."

"Curious? You were just curious! FOR OVER A YEAR MA NIGGA?! What man fucks another man out of curiosity for over a year?" I was really furious now. The only reason I ruined his wedding to Nikola's big ass was so we could be together. Now, he was telling me that we weren't going to be together because he was only fucking me out of curiosity. Oh, fuck no! That shit wasn't going to fly with me, and he knew it!

"I made a mistake with you. We," he said as he pointed from himself to me, "we made a mistake."

"I didn't make any damn mistake Charles. I love you!" I said. "Do you hear what I am saying to you? I AM IN LOVE WITH YOU!!"

"Keep your voice down!" he said through clenched teeth as he looked around the parking lot. "I don't need every fuckin' body in this damn town in my business again! You already have folks looking at me like I'm some kind of fruitcake..."

"Look Charles, I said what I said, and I meant it. I love you and I know that you love me too..."

"No, I don't."

"Don't say that! We've been through too much for you to still be denying your feelings for me!"

"I'm not denying anything. Look Jerry, I was confused. I thought that I wanted to be with you, but now that I don't have Nikola in my life anymore..." he paused and took a deep breath. "I miss her. I know it sounds strange, but I think that I'm in love with her."

What the fuck was his gay ass talking about? He wasn't in love with Shamu. He was in love with me. He told me that he loved me. He promised me that we'd be together forever. He promised. And now he was standing here telling me that he was in love with Rasputia! Oh, hell no! I did not work this hard to get this man to have him tell me that shit.

As I paced back and forth in front of him, trying to gather my bearings, all I saw was red.

"No, no, no! This can't be happening!" I said as the words he had just spoken to me sank in. "You love me! You told me that you loved me!"

"I'm sorry. I should've never said that to you."

"But you did... and I believed you!" I said as tears threatened to fall.

"I was confused," Charles said.

"Confused? You were confused? You're a grown ass man Charles who was loving and fucking on me for an entire year. That ain't confusion, honey!" I said as I twisted my neck and snapped my fingers.

"But I was. I thought I wanted to be with a man. I thought I wanted to be with you, but I don't. You brought excitement to my life when I most needed it. Nikola was busy planning the wedding and she didn't have time for me. You were there, and you made me feel special. You made time for me, and I thought that was what I wanted..."

"But now?"

"Now that Nikola has been gone from my life, I realize that I really love her. I love her and I wanna be with her. I don't know if she'll ever forgive me..."

WHAP!

That's right, I slapped the shit out of him! How dare he stand there and tell me that he loved her! How dare he tell me that he wanted her forgiveness so they can get back together! What about me? What the fuck was I supposed to do with all these feelings that I had for Charles? He led me to believe that if Nikola wasn't in the picture anymore that it would be just me and him. Now, she was out and had a man in her life. What the fuck was wrong with him?

"What did you do that for?" he asked as he rubbed his cheek.

I knew that shit hurt. Just because I sometimes acted like a princess, didn't make me one. At the end of the day, I was a grown ass man and I hit like one too.

"Don't you ever talk to me about the feelings you have for Orca!"

"Stop calling her names!" he said angrily.

Oh, it's like that? "Orca, Shamu, Rasputia, One Ton Wanda, Moby Dick, King Kongette!" I said. "You want me to keep going?"

"I'm leaving. Don't bother following me or I'll call the police, and have you arrested for trespassing!"

Oh, no he didn't just threaten to call the police on me! Well shit, let me give him a reason to call them.

"Call the po po's ho'! I don't give a fuck! I'll just tell them we're two lovers who got into a little spat!"

"We aren't lovers, and this isn't a spat! This is a breakup!"

"Oh right, because you were curious and confused!" I said.

"That's right! Now, stay the hell out of my life Jerry!"

"Hey Charles!"

He turned around in anger. "What?!"

"You know what curiosity did to the cat, don't you?" I asked as I flashed him a smile.

"Are you threatening me Jerry?" he asked.

I walked over to where he stood and looked him dead in his eyes. "I never make threats I can't follow through with. Consider this a promise. If you don't straighten your little tail out and make good on all those promises you made to me, I'm gonna kill you!"

"Boy, fuck you! You ain't got the balls to make a promise like that!"

"Oh, you think I'm playin' huh?" I grabbed him by the balls and squeezed as I whispered in his ear. "Try me. I pray to God that you try me!" I licked the side of his face then let him go.

He pushed me away from him and said, "Ain't nobody scared of you."

That was an outright lie because I could hear the fear in his voice. Shit, even his lips were trembling. I knew he was scared, and he had a right to be. Charles had promised me the world and I wanted it. Now, he was trying to get Nikola to take him back and I wasn't having that. He belonged to me. Whether he wanted it or not, we were going to be together.

"Okay. We'll see if you feel that way when the time comes for you to meet your maker." He didn't say anything as he rushed to his car. "Bye babe, I'll be seeing you!" I said I waved goodbye to him.

If he thought I was going to play with his ass, he had better think again. He'd better make the right decision because his sorry ass life depended on it. Now that he was gone, maybe I could sneak back in that club and have myself a good time. Shit, that music was going hard as fuck and I was feeling a little stressed. Dancing and liquor always put me in the mood for a good time and some good dick.

I headed back inside, but got stopped by the security guard.

"I thought I threw yo ass out!" he said as he mean mugged me.

I threw my hands up and plastered the biggest smile on my handsome face. "Look, Mr. Bouncer Man, I'm sorry about what happened earlier. I sent my friend home, so you won't get any more problems from me. All I wanna do is have a good time."

"If I catch you doing anything..."

"I just wanna grab a drink and hit the dance floor. Fa real, fa real!" I said.

"Aight, just remember what I said."

"Oh, I will. You so big and strong, I ain't even trying to fuck witchu like dat," I flirted.

Straight men always tried to get rid of us because they didn't want us to flirt with them. Sure enough, he let me in. I went straight to the bar, ordered a vanilla Crown on the rocks and headed to the dance floor. I had myself a good ol' time. Watching Nikola with her man helped me see that she really was done with Charles. She and that dude were all over each other. I knew he was fucking that big tiger pussy!

"Sshhiiid! I ain't mad atcha girl! You better stay away from Charles though... I know that!"

Chapter twelve

Charles

I had no idea Nikola would be at the club tonight. I just went there to have a conversation with Blaze so he could step back. I knew that she was starting to feel him, so if he didn't step away from her she'd never give me a chance to have her back. I know I sound stupid as fuck right now, but I really fucked up with Nikki. Once the wedding was called off and I was free to actually pursue a relationship with Jerry, I realized that wasn't what I wanted. I didn't want to be with Jerry like that anymore.

I know it sounds strange, but I thought I was gay. I had never been with a man before until I got with Jerry. I guess because Nikola was so busy planning the wedding, and Jerry making time for me had me confused. Now that Nikola was out of my life and had moved on, I was really missing her and the time we spent together. She always got me and made me laugh. She completed me.

Man, I wished I had realized that shit beforehand. Maybe I just had cold feet when it came down to the wedding. I should've discussed it with Nikki before I got involved with Jerry. I knew that was a mistake, but I still did it. Jerry had been there to listen to my troubles. He gave me advice and then put the moves on me. I didn't know what made me think that shit was okay, but it felt right. As long as I was running around on Nikki, my relationship with Jerry felt right. As soon as he outed me to everyone, it felt like I was losing myself. I tried to continue what he and I had started after Nikki said she wanted nothing to do with me, but it didn't work.

I didn't want to be with Jerry. I think it was the excitement of cheating on Nikola that made me think I wanted to be with him. I was confused as fuck once Nikki and I were over because I didn't want to be with Jerry anymore. I wanted Nikola back. Then I saw her with that dude at the restaurant that was like a kick in the stomach for me. When did she meet him?

I knew she hadn't been cheating on me. I thought she'd be home crying over me. I never thought she'd be out there dating someone else. I almost died when I saw her kissing all over that nigga at Copeland's. She always had a problem with public displays of affection, but so did I so we were comfortable just holding hands. But seeing her kissing that dude... what the hell?

I didn't know who the dude was, but she introduced me to him as Blaze, so it wasn't hard for me to find out that he owned the blues and jazz club on Decatur. I decided to go there and talk to him man to man. I figured if I told him I had made a mistake he'd understand and step aside. I needed him to do that so I could get my woman back. However, things didn't go as I thought they would. Instead of agreeing to step back so I could try to get Nikki back, he laughed at me. He told me that she didn't want me anymore... that she said she never wanted to be with me again.

I think I could've convinced him to leave her alone if Jerry hadn't shown up. When he showed up, he ruined everything. Then Nikola and Trinity showed up. I was so happy to see Nikola that I jumped out of my seat and practically ran to where she was standing. I just needed to speak to her about giving me another chance. I needed her to see the sincerity in my eyes and hear in my voice how sorry I was. I wanted to tell her that I made a huge mistake letting her go. I knew she wasn't in love with that dude already, so surely she wouldn't have a problem letting him go for me. We had too much history between us.

I was sure she had missed me just as much as I missed her, even though it was probably hard for her to admit that. Looking at her beautiful big marshmallow face, I could see that she was still angry with me. I didn't blame her. I had hoped that she would be able to find it in her heart to forgive me for embarrassing her that way. I never meant for her to find out the way that she did. Had it been up to me, she never would've found out. But Jerry had made that decision to tell her on his own. I had nothing to do with that.

Ever since the wedding was called off, Jerry had been pursuing me like crazy. He had pushed up on me several times, and I gave in to appease him. I was just tired of fighting him off. He expected us to be involved in a relationship though, but I wouldn't go that far... no matter how hard he pushed. I thought I wanted a relationship with him, but I really didn't. I wasn't gay, I was just confused. I wanted Nikola back in the worst way. I needed to have her back, but I knew it was going to take a miracle for her to forgive me and take me back.

When Jerry walked over to us and draped his arm across my shoulders, of course, I slapped it away. I wasn't into that shit... putting all my business out there for people to judge me. Nikola and Trinity seemed amused by the shit going down between me and Jerry. Blaze looked disgusted. Me, I was just livid that he would take shit this far in front of Nikola. My guess was that he was trying to make her jealous or stake his claim into me so she wouldn't want me.

Either way, he knew I hated when he behaved that way in public. Before I could even speak to Nikola in private, we were thrown out of the club. The way people were looking at us had me livid. I hated when people stared at me because I knew that they were thinking I was gay when I wasn't. I wished I had never messed with Jerry. He ruined my fucking life. I didn't get the promotion I had been working so hard for. I lost my girl to some other dude. And the whole town was looking at me as if I had committed some damn crime. Everything about my life sucked these days, and I had no one to blame but Jerry.

After I drove off, leaving him in the parking lot laughing, I sighed in relief. I'd never admit this shit to Jerry, but that nigga had me spooked. He had actually threatened my life, something he had never done before. As a matter of fact, no one had ever threatened to kill me before. I knew that he was mad about what I said to him, but to go that far and threaten my life was way out of line. I loved Nikola, but I'd never say some shit like that to her just to get her to come back to me. That was ridiculous!

With the way that Jerry was behaving, I wouldn't blame Nikola if she never took me back. I tried calling her after I left the club, of course she didn't answer. I'd give her a couple of days then call her again because we really needed to talk.

A couple of days passed since the incident at the club. I picked up the phone and called Nikola, but she didn't answer. I called a couple of hours later, and thankfully, she picked up.

"Hello," she answered sounding like she was out of breath.

"Nikola, can we talk?"

"Babe, hang up the phone!" I heard the dude in the background.

"Oh my God! Now really isn't a good time to talk," she said as she blew out a breath.

"Nikola please..."

"Oh shit! I gotta gooooooooo!"

CLICK!

"Was she having sex? Oh my God!"

I mean, if she was having sex, she should've never answered the damn phone. Who answers the phone during sex? That shit really hurt my feelings. The thought of Nikola in bed with that dude made me sick to my stomach... literally. I rushed to the bathroom to throw up. She hadn't even known him that long and she was giving him her goodies. Why would she do that when she knew I wanted to get back together with her?

I know I hurt her when Jerry brought our relationship to light on what was supposed to be our wedding day. But that didn't mean she should fall in bed with some random dude. The dude looked like he was related to Ice Cube in the *Boyz in the Hood* movie. How could she be seriously interested in that dude? She was too classy to be involved with a nigga like that. He was going to bring her down and she knew it.

It was best for her to get out of it while she still could. I still couldn't believe she answered that phone while she was having sex. The sex must not have been that good for her to be picking up the phone and shit. I decided that I'd go to her office and speak to her because it seemed as though that was the only time I'd get to have a conversation with her.

So, the next day, I went to work, but during my lunch break, I decided to pop over to Nikola's office. I picked up some food from Chili's along the way because I knew she liked their pasta. Her office was only 15 minutes away from mine, so it didn't take me that long to get there. I wished I had thought of that sooner. I grabbed the Chili's bag and headed to the elevator. Her office was on the fourth floor of the huge glass building. When the elevator dinged, I stepped in and pressed the number four button.

When it came to a stop, I exited and made my way to the receptionist's desk.

"Good afternoon Mr. Harmon, how may I help you?" asked Lanell. She knew who I was because she had been working here since before me and Nikola started dating.

"Hey Lanell, is Nikola in her office?"

"I believe so."

"Is she busy?"

"I think she's preparing for a meeting this afternoon. Would you like me to let her know that you're here?"

"I'd actually like to surprise her if that's okay," I said.

"Hmm, I don't know. Considering how the wedding went down..."

"Please Lanell, that was months ago. We've made our peace with it and we're still friends, plus I brought lunch. You know how she loves her pasta from Chili's," I begged.

"Okay, but if she gets mad, I'm gonna tell her that I wasn't aware you went in there because I had stepped away from my desk," she relented.

"It'll be fine. I promise."

I went to the door and knocked. I didn't wait for her to say come in. I just let myself in. She was on the phone when I walked in, and judging from the smile on her face, I already knew who she was talking to.

"What the fuck?" she said as she stared at me. "Babe let me call you back."

She hung the phone up as she eyeballed me. "Surprise!" I said.

Rolling her eyes and shucking her teeth, she asked, "What the hell are you doing here Charles? I thought I made it clear to you that I wasn't interested in anything you had to offer or discuss."

"Nikola please... I brought your favorite pasta!" I said as I held up the Chili's to go bag.

"I don't care if that pasta came with Jesus and one of the disciples. Why are you here?"

"I thought we could talk about that over lunch."

"I already ate a salad."

"Salad? You hate salads," I replied.

"That was before. So, what do you want? I have a meeting in a couple of hours, so say what you need to say and leave."

"Okay, first I'd like to apologize to you for things ending the way that they did..."

She played an imaginary violin on her shoulder and said, "You already said that. I couldn't care less about your apology then and I could care even less about it now."

"Humph! I made a mistake Nikola..."

"A mistake?"

"Yes, not marrying you was the worst thing I could've done. I miss you," I said as I walked closer to her desk.

"Uh uh, before you get to close, I'm gonna stop you." She stood up and came around the desk to where I was standing. I hadn't noticed it before, but she looked like she had lost a little weight. "I don't know where this missing me bullshit is coming from..."

"It's coming from deep within my heart. I really miss you. I miss talking to you, I miss laughing with you... I basically miss everything about you. I'm sorry I've been such a jerk..."

"Actually, your being a jerk worked out fine. If you hadn't been screwing Jerry, I never would've met Lincoln..."

"Who? I thought you were dating Blaze," I said.

I mean, good Lord! How many niggas did I have to compete with? First, Blaze and now this Lincoln dude.

"That's his real name, not that it's any of your business," she said.

Dammit! I had totally forgotten that nigga's name was Lincoln.

"Oh," I simply replied.

"Anyway, meeting Lincoln was a great thing for me. He's kind, gentle, and he motivates me to be a better person."

"I never thought there was anything wrong with you."

"Yea, well, Lincoln did. A woman as big as I am was setting myself up for health issues, a whole bunch of them. Lincoln is showing me how to properly exercise and diet."

"I would've helped you with that Nikola, but I was afraid you would think I wasn't accepting you for who you were."

"See... and that's the difference between you and Lincoln. He doesn't care if it's something that I wanna hear or not. He keeps it real with me. At first, I was upset because I felt like he was calling me fat. But then he listed all the things that could go wrong with my health. He pointed out that besides the high blood pressure and high cholesterol that I already have, I could get diabetes and other issues. You see, he's isn't saying that he doesn't care about me for who I am. He's just saying that he wants me to take better care of myself, so I'll be around longer. I needed to hear that," she said with a smile.

"Wow! But if I would've told you that you needed to lose weight, you would've complained about me not loving you for who you are."

"Maybe it was your delivery. You never mentioned anything about my health. The couple of times you mentioned my weight being a problem, you asked me if I wasn't uncomfortable being that size."

"And you almost slapped the shit out of me!"

"Because your delivery was all wrong. If you would've said something like, 'Babe I'm worried about you. I don't want you having any health issues because of your weight', I probably would've been more receptive."

"Have you lost any weight? Or is it just shifting around?"

"No, it's not just shifting around. I went from 379 to 363. I have a long way to go, but I'm gonna do it. Now, if you'll excuse me. I have to prepare for this meeting," she said as she walked closer to the door.

"Please Nikola, I'll work out with you! I'll do all the things you need me to do for you. I just want another chance," I said.

"HA! Let me make something perfectly clear to you Charles. I never want to be with you again. You and I are done. You're lucky I hadn't gotten no STDs from you because we really would've had problems. I wouldn't take you back for three good reasons. Number one, you cheated on me. I was a good woman to you, but you cheated on me. Number two, you cheated on me with a man. You can't be trusted with men or women around..."

"I was wrong for doing that! I never should've cheated on you with Jerry. I don't even know why I did it because I'm not even gay!"

"Now that is some bullshit if I've ever heard it. Please don't ever repeat that shit again. How is it you don't think you're gay when you have been getting it on with a man? Never mind! Forget I asked because that is not my business! What you do and who you do it with is between you and that man or woman," she said as she shook her head and waved her hands. "The third reason I'd never be with you is because I found someone who makes me happy... happier than I ever thought possible."

"Nikola he's not the right man for you," I said.

"That's not your business! Look, obviously things aren't going the way that you thought they would with Jerry. But that has nothing to do with me. Y'all need to work that shit out because you and I are done. We will never be together again. Oh, and you don't need to go by Lincoln's club to talk to him about me either. Even if I wasn't with him, I still wouldn't be with you. You're gay or bisexual, whatever. Until you're able to accept and deal with your sexuality, you'll never be happy. I suggest you go find out who you really are before you try to get involved with anyone else... man or woman."

"Don't say that. I just made a mistake."

"A mistake would've been cheating on me with a woman. At least I could compete with someone who had the same anatomy as me. You don't mistakenly cheat on your woman with a man! Nah, that was some deliberate shit and something I can't or won't compete with. Now, you've said your peace, I heard you out, now you have to get the hell out of my office!" she said in an agitated voice. "Now, I'm trying to put an end to this shit in a nice manner. If I have to call security to escort you out..."

"You don't have to do that. I'll leave," I said sadly. I placed the bag of food on the round table in her office and turned to leave.

"Uh, you're forgetting something," she said as she picked up the bag.

"I bought that for you and I to have lunch. If you won't have lunch with me, maybe you can eat lunch with Lanell."

"No can do, boo. I just told you that I ate already. You can take your little bag back to work with you and share it with someone else," she said.

Damn. Why was she being so rude?

"But it's your favorite."

"But I ate already! Just take it with you please!"

I took the bag from her and walked toward the door. The last thing I wanted was for her to call security on me. It just wasn't that serious.

Before I walked out, I left her with some parting words.

"When that man leaves you high and dry, feel free to call me. I'll always be there for you because mark my words... he ain't who you think he is. Thugs like him always have some excess baggage somewhere. Sooner or later, his secrets will come to light," I said.

"Secrets or no secrets, I'll never go back to you. Now, goodbye!"

There was nothing left for me to say. I left without saying another word. I don't know much about that dude, but I knew she would need me sooner or later. And guess who was gon be waiting on her... ME!

Once I got downstairs, I stepped off the elevator and had another problem. I looked up and there was Jerry with the most extreme expression I had ever seen on his face. What the fuck was he doing here?

Chapter thirteen

Jerry

Of course, I still had the tracking device on Charles. It was the only way I was going to be able to figure out what he was up to. So, you can imagine my surprise when I followed that little dot all the way to the office building Nikola worked out of. What the hell was he doing here? I already had an idea, but I wasn't going to speculate. I was going to use my inside voice and curb my attitude until we spoke.

So, I made my way to the building and parked my car. Then I headed inside and waited. There was no reason for me to go upstairs to Nikola's office because I knew that's where he was. I decided to take a seat in the lobby and wait. Five minutes after I got there, he came strolling out of the elevator with a Chili's to go bag. So, he brought her big ass some lunch huh? I sure hoped he brought her a damn salad because that's the only thing her big fat ass should've been eating from Chili's.

As soon as he saw me, he rolled his eyes. He didn't say shit to me as he walked pass me and headed for the door. Oh no, his ass didn't just ignore me. I walked at full speed behind him trying to catch up to him before he had a chance to haul his ass outta here. I quickly followed outside and matched his steps.

"So, you're just going to ignore me like you didn't see me sitting there? Is that what we're doing now… ignoring each other?"

"Why are you here? How did you know that I was even over here?"

"I came here to find out why you were here and how I found out isn't your concern! So, tell me, exactly what are you doing here?"

"My business is my business and I don't have to tell you what I do!"

"You're right! You don't have to tell me shit because I already know why you're here. I just wanna know why?"

"Why what?" he asked as he rolled his eyes and let out an exasperated breath.

"Why were you here visiting Nikola? Did you bring her lunch too? You could've brought lunch to me, but you chose to bring it to her instead! Would you like to tell me why?" I asked.

"I don't need to tell you shit! You are not responsible for me!"

"You're right. I just wanna know what happened between the two of you!"

"Nothing, alright! Not a damn thing! We didn't even have lunch!" he said.

"Why didn't you have lunch? Did she throw you out or what?"

"None of your damn business!"

"None of my damn business?! I risked everything to be with you! I even lost my job because of you!" I fussed.

And it was true. Once I came out and said what I said about me and Charles, one of us had to go. There was a strict no fraternization policy in place, so rather than let us both go, they chose to just terminate one of us... ME! Because I was in a lower level position and Charles was up there, they chose to let me go. I didn't even get a warning or nothing. When I reported to work the Monday, I was called into the executive vice president's office where he promptly fired me. I got a severance package, but because I was being terminated instead of laid off, it wasn't that much.

I had done it all for love. I thought Charles would run into my loving arms and everything would be hunky dory once he was free, but that wasn't how things worked out. The more I pushed for us to be in a monogamous relationship or hell, any relationship these days, the more he pushed back. He kept running to Nikola's fat ass and it had me wondering if she had voodoo on him. I mean, what man would come out of the closet, then turn around and try to get back with the woman he didn't marry?

Charles was playing a dangerous game that I didn't like, and something was gonna have to give. I was losing my patience with him. We were supposed to be off somewhere enjoying each other and the fact that we didn't have to creep around anymore. But all he was worried about was getting Nikola's chunky monkey ass back.

What the hell did she have that I didn't besides a mountain of cat? Her cat was so big, I'm surprised Charles was still standing here today. In my eyes, as slim as he was, he should've fallen in a long time ago. Look at me, I was a total catch with my chocolatey morsel ass. I looked exactly like a Hershey's kiss, Muah! I was slim, but not too slim. I had deep dimples, a beautiful smile, good wavy hair, and I carried myself in a way that made anyone turn to look at me... men and women. I also smelled good. Hell let's go one step further and say I smelled heavenly. I was the epitome of a beautiful, gay man and I was proud of myself and my sexuality.

But this nigga here... he was ruining my perfect blood pressure with his silliness.

He stopped walking and so did I. I crossed my arms over my chest because I did not want to go to jail. I knew if he said some slick shit, I was gon' let it rip on his ass and that would land me right in the slammer. Jail wasn't for me. I was too cute and sexy to be dressed in some damn orange jumpsuit, or worst the black and white stripes. Eww! Talk about a fashion faux pas!

"I didn't ask you to open your mouth and tell the world that we were sleeping together. As a matter of fact, I begged you not to say anything. I was about to get a promotion... one you know I had been working my ass off for. All I had to do was marry Nikola and I would've been making $150,000 a year! If anybody ruined something, it was you! You made the decision to out us in front of the whole town. You, not me! So, if you're looking for someone to blame for your ass getting fired, look in the mirror buddy!"

"How was I supposed to just stand there and watch the man that I love marry someone else? I just couldn't do it!" I cried.

"And that's your problem! I don't love you Jerry, I probably never did. I thought I did because you were there for me when no one else was, but I don't. I should've just talked to Nikola and let her know that I was having cold feet. I should've talked to her about my feelings, but you swooped in and took advantage of my vulnerability. You seduced me into having sex with you..."

What in the hail Mary full of grace shit is this nigga talking about? I seduced him? I didn't need to seduce him because he was already open to getting it on with me. I took advantage of him. That almost sounded like rape and I ain't never had to rape anybody baby.

"Wait one minute there, homeboy! I did NOT, I repeat, DID NOT take advantage of you! You wanted me just as badly as I wanted you. And furthermore, what's all this shit about you never loving me? You said you loved me more than once. Those words didn't just accidentally fall off your tongue one night in the heat of the moment. No siree Bob! You said that on more than one occasion, so don't be trying to put all that shit on me like you didn't know what you were doing or saying!"

"This isn't the time or place for us to be having this discussion!" he said as people passed by looking at us.

"Why not? BECAUSE OF THESE NOSEY ASS WHITE FOLKS ALL IN OUR BUSINESS! FUCK THEM! I'M SURE THEY SAW LOVERS QUARREL BEFORE!" I shouted.

"We are not lovers!" Charles said through clenched teeth.

"The only reason we ain't been fucking is because you've been going through some kind of crisis or something! That big whale of a tail bitch does not want you! She's told you that enough times. Why hasn't it sunk in yet?"

"She's gonna come around. She just needs more time," he reasoned.

"She'll never come around... not with that beautiful Adonis looking thang she's been fucking."

"Shut the fuck up Jerry!"

"The truth hurts, doesn't it? That girl will never come back to you. The dude she's fucking with probably has a longer dick than yours. He probably hits spots she didn't even know she had because of all those ruffles on her belly..." I said and cracked up laughing.

"For your information, she's lost some weight. She's eating salads and exercising. She's on the path to being healthier..."

"Umph! Another thing she can probably thank Mandingo for! See, she's doing all that shit without you! She don't want you no more, but I do. I don't care how short or long your dick is because it fits perfectly in my a..."

"Shut up Jerry! Look, I gotta get back to work. Stop following me around like a lost dog and get you some business!" he said.

"You are my business Charles. Until you act right, I'm going to show up everywhere you go."

"How do you know where I am? How did you know that I was here? Are you tracking my iPhone?"

"Hell naw! Ain't nobody got time for all that shit!" I said as I waved him off. "I just know, okay? Call it a man's intuition."

"I call it stalking and you better stop."

"Um hm, I'll stop when you bring yo ass home!"

"You're crazy!"

"You have no idea how cray cray I can actually be. Trust me, you ain't seen that side of me yet, and you don't want to. I'm not going to keep playing this game with you Charles," I said.

"Then leave me alone!" he said and stomped off.

"I'll leave you alone alright," I said as I turned and walked back to the building. It was time for me and Rasputia to have a little talk.

I hit the elevator to take me to the fourth floor. As I rode the elevator, I hummed 2Pac's song, *I Ain't Mad At Cha*. I loved that song and had recently started listening to it every day. When the elevator dinged, I got off and headed to the receptionist's area.

"Good afternoon, how may I help you?" greeted the receptionist.

"Good afternoon to you," I said, sounding a lot cheerier than I felt. "I'm here to see Raspu... gotdammit! I almost forgot where I was!" I cracked my own self up sometimes. "I'm here to see Nikola Anderson please."

"She's in a meeting right now. Would you like to leave a message?"

"No, I'll wait," I said.

"I'm not sure how long her meeting will run."

"I don't mind waiting. I have nothing else on my agenda for the day, so it's no biggie. Carry on," I said as I waved her off and took a seat in the lobby.

I sat there scrolling through my Facebook and Instagram pages for about an hour. Then I checked the tracker to make sure that Charles was back at work... he was. About 20 minutes later, here comes Rasputia. She did look like she had lost two pounds, so I wasn't impressed.

"Any calls while I was out?" she asked the girl.

The girl handed her a couple of pink slips and said, "Someone has been waiting to speak with you."

"Who?" She pointed to me. I stood up and did a curtsy. She rolled her eyes and walked over to me. "What do you want Jerry? I am not in the mood for your shit today."

"I just would like to have a conversation with you. This shouldn't take longer than a couple of minutes," I bartered.

"C'mon."

I followed her lumpy ass to her office. Her feet looked way too big and fat for those heels. It almost looked like a busted can of biscuits had been placed in those shoes. The heels looked like they were screaming for help as they struggled to carry her big ass body. Someone her size should definitely look into the benefits of wearing flats. She sat behind her desk looking like an overweight Precious. I sat in the chair right across from her.

"What can I do for you?"

"Why was Charles here?" I asked, getting right to the damn point.

"How do you know that he was here?"

"Because I saw him here. What was he doing here?"

"Well, if you saw him here, why didn't you ask him why he was here?"

"I did, but he gave me this song and dance about wanting to have lunch with you, but you wouldn't."

"That's actually true. He did come here to have lunch with me, but I told him that I wasn't interested."

"So, he was here for half an hour doing what exactly?"

"Oh no!" she said as she stood up from her chair. I could almost hear the heels of her shoes crying as she walked over to the other side of the desk. "I am not going to do this shit with you. I don't know what you and Charles got going on and I don't care. What I need for both of y'all to do is get y'all shit together and stay out of my life!"

"Did you tell Charles that?"

"I did. Look, I want nothing to do with Charles anymore. The fact that he cheated on me with you let's me know that I'm not the right person for him. Besides, I already have a man!"

"Oh yes! I saw that hunk of a man that you call yours..."

"Good, and you don't need to make a play for him because he's all about the women. Well, me. So, whatever is going on between you and Charles, y'all need to fix it and leave me alone!"

"I just came down here to speak with you because I'm tired of him disrespecting me!"

"What does that have to do with me? The way I see it, you both disrespected me when y'all started sleeping together. Did either of you care about how I would feel when I found out? Obviously not! Because you ruined my wedding with your little announcement!"

"But aren't you glad I said something? I mean, wasn't it better that you learned before marrying him than after," I asked.

"Oh yes! You did me a huge favor..."

"You're welcome."

"Now, do me another favor."

"What's that?"

"Get the hell out of my office and don't come back!" she said as she opened the door.

My mouth flew open. No, this Miss Piggy looking bitch did not just open the door to throw me out of her office. I stood up and walked over to the door.

"You know, that dress is too tight for your fat ass. You need a 30 instead of a 28. And those shoes aren't doing your feet any justice. It looks like you're baking banana bread in those too small shoes..."

"GET OUT!!" she yelled angrily.

With two snaps in a circle, I sashayed my cute ass right up outta there. I was only trying to give her a few fashion tips, but apparently, she took it wrong. "By the way, that foundation color is all wrong for your skin tone. You're too dark for that Flintstone color!"

She pushed me out and locked her door. Dammit! She had better lock that fucking door because I would've gone back in there and... never mind. I held my head up high and walked out like Naomi Campbell on the runway.

"Fuck Rasputia!"

Now, to figure out what I'm going to do about Charles' and his disrespectful ass.

Chapter fourteen

Nikola

"Ugh! The nerve of that pipsqueak!" I yelled as I picked up my phone and dialed Lanell's extension.

"Yes, Miss Anderson."

"Lanell, why did you let Charles back here? Why didn't you at least ask me if I wanted to see him? Were you not at my almost wedding three months ago!"

"Yes, Miss Anderson, but I thought..."

"You thought what? When someone comes to this office and they don't have an appointment and I'm not expecting them, you're supposed to check with me first!" I barked.

I was angry because Charles had been popping up every damn where lately and I wasn't having it. I was done with him and I couldn't understand why he didn't get that. He had made his choice. Now, all of a sudden it was a mistake. I didn't give a shit about the fact that he made a "mistake." What kind of mistake lands another man's dick in your ass? What kind of mistake puts your dick in his ass? That was some bullshit!

"I'm sorry Miss Anderson. It won't happen again," Lanell apologized.

"Make sure that it doesn't. If Charles comes back around here, have him promptly escorted out of this building," I warned.

"Yes ma'am."

I ended the call with her and called Lincoln back.

"Hey babe," I cooed into the phone when he answered.

"Hey, I can't talk right now," he said abruptly.

"Oh, I'm sorry."

"No problem. I'll hit you back later."

With that he ended the call. I looked at my phone feeling a bit deflated. Like damn.

Blaze had been out of town for the past few days and I missed him. He was in Houston on business, or so he said. I suspected that he was also visiting his son when he went out there. I had no problem with that because that was his little boy before I was his woman. He deserved to visit with his son because I was sure the little boy missed him. However, I had the feeling that the baby's mama, his ex-wife may be trying to sink her claws back into him.

I didn't really know her or anything about her. All I knew was that their relationship went sour. I didn't even know her name, how long they were married before they divorced… nothing. I didn't ask questions about her because I didn't want to pry too much into his personal business.

I just felt that if he wanted me to know things, he'd tell me. After all, we've only been dating for a few months. I didn't have the right to question him about his past that way. Maybe sometime later on, but not now. I called Trinity because I needed to talk to her about what just happened. I was just feeling some kind of way about that phone call. I couldn't explain it, but it left me feeling pretty empty.

"Hey BFF, what you up to?" Trinity greeted.

"Nothing."

"Why you sound like you lost your best friend though?"

"Girl, so much has happened."

"Do tell."

"Well, first I was talking to Lincoln cause you know he's in Houston right?"

"Yea, when's he coming back?"

"In a couple of days, I think."

"So, how did the conversation go?"

"Well, we were having a great conversation until Charles walked in."

"What the fuck?" she exclaimed. "What the hell did he want?"

"Girl, he came by to give me this bullshit excuse about how he made a mistake with Jerry. About how he was wrong and wants me back... yada, yada, yada!"

"Wow! He just doesn't know how to take no for an answer, huh?"

"I'm sayin'! He's definitely trippin'. I told him that sleeping with a man wasn't a mistake. It was a conscious decision that he made and for that, we would never get back together."

"Wow! So, then what did he say?"

"Then he started talking about Lincoln and how he wasn't the man for me. Talking about how thugs like him always have secrets."

"Like he hadn't hid the biggest secret ever revealed for almost a damn year!" Trinity chimed in.

"For real! He has a lot of nerve talking about the next man!" I said.

"That dude is crazy. I wonder if you should put a restraining order on him because he's a borderline stalker these days."

"I don't think it's that serious to get a restraining order. He knows now that there is no chance of us ever getting together again. And Lanell knows that it's her ass if she ever just sends him through without checking with me. As a matter of fact, I told her not to ever let him in."

"Right! I hope you told her to call security for his ass!"

"I did," I confirmed.

"Good for you. He's not going to do anything to me. I mean, I'm not afraid of him because all he's doing is aggravating me and getting on my damn nerves," I expressed.

"I'm sure he is. So, is that why you sound so sad?"

"No, so after I threw Charles out, I called Lincoln back..."

"I'm so used to you saying Blaze. It's gonna take me some time to accept that his real name is Lincoln," she laughed.

"Well, anyway, so I called him, and he blew me off," I said sadly.

"What do you mean he blew you off? Did you guys argue about Charles?"

"No, I didn't even get a chance to tell him that Charles had stopped by. When I say he blew me off, I mean he blew me off! He answered the phone, I said hey baby. Then he said hey, I can't talk now and hung up!"

My feelings were really hurt because I took a chance letting Lincoln in my space. I didn't know what was going on with Lincoln. I just hoped that he wasn't blowing me off to have sex with his ex-wife.

"Well, you did say that he was out of town on business. Maybe he was in a business meeting," she reasoned.

"I don't know. It was just strange, and it left me feeling so empty," I said.

"I'm sorry boo. I'm sure he was just busy. I wouldn't read too much into it because he was probably just in the middle of something."

"Yea, that's what I'm afraid of."

"What do you mean?"

"You do know his son and ex-wife live out there, right?"

"Yea, and?"

"So, what if he couldn't talk to me cuz he was fucking her?"

"Wow! Look girl, that's reaching pretty high. I mean, who has time to answer the phone when they're having sex?" Trinity reasoned.

"Well, I did the other day when Charles called..."

"No, you didn't!"

"Yes, I did! I wanted him to hear me so he could know that I really moved on. I thought that would keep him from contacting me again, but then he showed up here today."

"Right. That's some funny shit, but you can't judge Blaze like that. If you're going to give him a chance, give him a chance without restrictions," Trinity said.

"What restrictions?"

"If you're harboring trust issues from your past relationships, you shouldn't be messing with Blaze. Whatever y'all have going on won't work if you don't trust him."

"Do you blame me for having trust issues?"

"No, of course, I don't. I just want you to be happy sis. You won't find happiness if you don't open your heart to trust again."

"You do realize just three and a half months ago I was standing at the altar to marry someone else, right?"

"Yes. So, do you think that your relationship with Blaze is too soon?" she inquired. "Because if that's the case, pump the brakes on it. Tell him that y'all have been moving too fast and you wanna slow things down a bit."

"I don't know what I want Trinity. I really like Blaze, but you're right. Maybe I did move too fast with him. I was trying to have a friends with benefits type thing, but my heart won't let me keep it at that."

"That's the thing with us women. When we have emotional connections with someone, it's hard to stay in the friend zone. You thought you had a handle on things with Blaze, but then your heart got involved. You'll just have to either trust him or let him go boo."

"I don't know what to do."

"Well, you said he wasn't gonna be back for a couple of more days, so sleep on it. Think about what you want and where you want things to go with him. I mean, y'all only been kicking it for three months or so. The relationship is still fresh."

"Thanks Trinity. You always seem to know exactly what I need to hear."

"I ain't your bestie for nothing sis. But can I say something before you kick Blaze to the curb?"

"Sure, and no one said I was kicking him to the curb."

"Right, but you're contemplating it, so... But anyway, think about how he makes you feel and what's he's brought to your life. Since you've met him, you've even lost a few pounds. He cares about you, your health and your weight. And I don't mean that in an ugly way either. What I'm saying is weigh the positives and negatives and if the you feel you'd be better off without him, then tell him you want to be just friends. Cut out the quality time. Definitely quit having sex with him. Just take the time to be by yourself and figure out what you want."

"Okay, cool. I can do that," I said.

"Good. I'll talk to you soon. Love you," Trinity said.

"Love you too sis."

I ended the call and had exactly 20 minutes to get my things in order for my meeting. I had created a website for one of my clients and I knew he was going to love it.

Imagine my surprise when I got back from my meeting and found Jerry waiting for me. Oh God! First Charles retarded ass and now him. Why me God? Why me?

To have him come to my place of business and question me about my ex was crazy. I mean, wasn't he the one who ruined my big day because he wanted the world to know that he and Charles were involved? Now that I was done with Charles, I couldn't for the life of me understand why the two of them wouldn't leave me alone. For him to come and ask me why his lover was visiting me should have been a question for Charles. He shouldn't have questions for me about anything to do with them and their relationship.

And then for him to be so insulting to me when I asked him to leave, ugh! I had never been ugly or disrespectful to Jerry... ever! I guess I was going to have to put him on my list to keep out also. I didn't have time for them and their bullshit. I just wanted some peace. Of course, I called Trinity and gave her the rundown. She was just as pissed off as I was. She agreed that I should put him on the list for Lanell to contact security if he ever showed up again. I did that as soon as I hung up the phone with her. I really wished that Lincoln would call. He would know what to say to make me feel better and ease my mind.

Well, I didn't hear from Lincoln that evening or the next day. I decided I wasn't going to say anything. I was just going to wait to hear from him. Wait to find out what he had to say when he returned. If he calls me fine. If he didn't, it is what it is. But one thing was for certain... I wasn't going to lose myself in a man again.

If things didn't go good with Lincoln, we had some good times. I'd just leave it at that.

So, Lincoln hit me up two days later, which was Friday afternoon. I was hoping to hear from him but had it on my mind that I wouldn't. I mean, I hadn't heard from him since that afternoon, so I was worried. However, I wasn't going to be one of those clingy women who called every time I didn't hear from him. Since he had said he would call me back, I just patiently waited for him to do just that.

"Hey," I answered.

"Hey there Nikki, how are you?"

"I'm good. How about you?"

"I'm straight."

"That's good. Are you back in town?"

"Yea, I got in a couple of hours ago. I had so much shit to do cuz I've been gone for a while, ya know?"

"Yea, I feel ya," I responded.

"So, I was wondering what you were doing later."

"Oh, I've had a long day. I'm going home, jump in the shower and get to sleep," I said.

I wasn't that tired, but that's what I told him because now that he was back, I just didn't want to make myself readily available like I had been doing. Maybe that was why he took so long to call me back and shit. I hadn't made him work hard enough for me. So, now, he was going to have to put in work if he wanted to be with me.

"Oh, okay. I was hoping that I'd be able to see you. I missed you while I was gone."

"Aw, that's sweet. I missed you too, but I've been up since early this morning and I haven't been sleeping well..."

"Is everything alright? That nigga ain't been bothering you huh?" he asked.

"No, I haven't heard from him since he dropped by the other day."

"He dropped by? You didn't tell me that."

Humph! How did he want me to tell him when he was just returning my call?

"It wasn't a big deal. He dropped by, I threw him out and haven't heard from him since."

"Well, if you need me to have another talk with him..."

"No, that won't be necessary. I think he got the picture," I said.

"He better get it!"

"Look Lincoln, I'm glad you're back safe and sound, but I have some work I need to finish up before I leave for the weekend. I'll holla at you tomorrow," I said.

"Are you okay? I mean, are we good?"

"Yea, why do you ask?"

"I'on know. It just seems like there's something different in your voice. I just can't put my finger on it."

"I'm good, just tired," I lied.

"Okay. Well, holla tomorrow. Get some rest."

"I will, thanks."

We ended the call and I sat back in my chair. Well, at least he had finally made it back home. I guess I'd give him a call and see where things could go from here.

So, the next day, I called Lincoln to talk.

"Hello," he answered in a groggy tone. It sounded as if he was still sleeping.

"Hi, did I catch you at a bad time?"

"Nah, it's cool. How are you?"

"Good. How bout you?"

"I'm straight. I miss you."

"Do you really?"

"Yes, why would you question that?" he asked.

"Because I haven't heard from you much since you've been gone."

"I'm sorry about that. I kind of got swept up in some shit from my past with my old crew. It was mad crazy out there."

"Well, I'm glad you made it home safe."

"Me too," he said.

I never actually knew what he did for a living before he moved to New Orleans. I didn't know if I really wanted to know. I mean, if he wanted me to know, he would've told me right? My guess was that he was running from something. But what do I know?

"So, when can I see you?" I asked.

"Well, I have to go by the club later and I have a few errands to run. I mean, if you wanna come over to the club..."

"I don't know. We haven't seen each other in days, so I was hoping for some alone time to discuss things."

"Yea, well, maybe tomorrow."

"Yea, maybe."

"Look, I gotta get up and take a shower. I'll hit you up a little later," he said.

"Okay. Take care," I said and ended the call.

What was going on with him? He just sounded so strange lately. The more I thought about it, the more I thought that maybe it wouldn't be a bad idea to go to the club. I mean, we needed to have a conversation about where this relationship was going. If I was wasting my time, it's best I found out sooner rather than later.

Several hours later, I made my way to the club. I was anxious and excited to see Lincoln. I wondered if it was a good idea to just show up. But then again, he had invited me there. It wasn't as if I was just showing up without him knowing. I walked in and the club was packed as always. After my eyes scanned the club for a few minutes, I finally spotted him sitting at a table with a female.

The two of them were talking and laughing, so it kinda had me feeling some kind of way. I mean, could she be the reason I hadn't been seeing or hearing from him that much? Shit, if she was, I was going to find out.

I walked over there on wobbly legs, my heart beating at a rate of speed I wasn't used to. Lincoln spotted me before I got to the table and he walked over to me. "Hey," he said nervously.

"Hey yourself," I greeted.

He hugged me swiftly. "I thought you weren't coming."

"I changed my mind. I thought that since you missed me, it was better to see you here than not at all."

"Right. Are you thirsty?"

"No, not really. Who's the girl you were talking to?" I asked as I looked pass him at the woman still sitting at the table.

She looked at me questioningly and walked over to us. It wasn't until she stood next to Lincoln did I notice that she was pregnant. "What's going on?" I asked as my lips trembled.

"Blaze, whose she?" the woman asked.

"Yea Blaze, tell her who I am," I said as I looked at the woman.

"Nikola, I didn't want you to find out this way. I was gonna tell you, but I didn't know how," Lincoln said.

"You were going to tell me what Lincoln?"

"Oh wow! She knows your real name," the woman said. "This must be serious."

"Who are you?" I asked as I stared at her.

"I'm Tricia, Blaze's wife."

"You mean, his ex-wife, right?"

"No, we aren't divorced. Blaze, you told her we were divorced?"

My mouth suddenly went dry. It was like my tongue was stuck to the roof of my mouth and I couldn't get it to work. Lincoln was married. How could he be married? He told me he was married before, but he left out the part about still being married. Why wouldn't he tell me about his wife?

"So, this is your wife? Is she carrying your baby too?" I asked.

Lincoln stood there as if he were stuck on stupid. What the hell? He had better say something. "Lincoln, I asked you a question!"

"Yea, this is my wife and she is carrying my baby, but it's not what you think."

"It's not what I think? You told me you were married... WERE MARRIED! That means you were married before, but you're not now!"

"Nikola..."

WHAP!

"Fuck you Lincoln, Blaze or whoever the fuck you are! Fuck you! I never wanna see you again!" I said as I rushed out of the club.

God really must hate me to keep doing this to me! I got in my car and couldn't hold back the tears any longer. I cried as if I had lost my best friend. "WHY GOD?! I JUST WANNA KNOW WHY YOU KEEP DOING THIS TO ME?!!"

I mean, don't I deserve some happiness too? What's wrong with me that I can't be happy? What did I ever do that was so bad that I can't find happiness?

"Please God, just take me now! I'm ready to die because living here on this earth has caused me nothing, but pain from the time I was born. I just want you to stop my heart from beating, so I never experience this type of pain again. Please God, if you love me you'll take me away from all of this hurt!" I begged.

Even though Lincoln and I hadn't been together that long, I had still opened myself up to him. I had told him about Charles, about Miles... I had even told him about my mother. He hadn't told me much about himself, but he seemed a little guarded. I had hoped with time he'd be able to open up to me too. But now, I know why he didn't open up to me. He was hiding a whole wife who was pregnant with his kid.

I just wanted God to take away the pain...

To be continued...

CPSIA information can be obtained
at www.ICGtesting.com
Printed in the USA
LVHW031602210519
618617LV00002B/345/P